The Stars Burn Bright

LYNDA TOMALIN

Published by GlitterInk Press Ltd – New Zealand

ISBN: 978-1-99-118051-3 (NZ Edition Paperback)
ISBN: 978-1-99-118050-6 (POD Paperback)
ISBN: 978-1-99-118053-7 (Epub)
ISBN: 978-1-99-118052-0 (Kindle)

Cover Design by Jennifer Rackham
Editing and proofreading by
Bellbird Words Proofreading, Editing, and Writing Services

www.lyndatomalinauthor.com

For Ciff,

For giving me my own love story

x

Chapter One

ESSIE

MY BLOOD BOILS and a red haze settles in front of my eyes as the words I've just heard echo through my mind.

"She's your kid sister. Don't be gross."

I know the voice, even if I haven't heard it in months.

Jackson "Jax" Sherwood.

My brother's best friend and, as of this very moment, officially my arch nemesis.

I take a deep breath, smooth down the bottle-green skirt of my school uniform and saunter into the kitchen.

My brother, David, looks up at me, then glances away, barely acknowledging my arrival. Jax sits at the counter, his light brown hair falling into his eyes. He lifts his chin at me, a silent form of hello.

I dump my lunch containers on the bench and try to ignore him, try to convey my disdain through a wicked twist of my lips.

"Hi," I say instead, my voice thin and reedy. I hate myself almost as much as I hate him. I stack the containers in the dishwasher before Mum can come home and complain I've left a mess. I feel bad for them, the way I'm slamming them into the rack.

"How was school?" Jax asks, his eyes sparking with amusement.

I huff a breath, an angry sigh. "Fine." Then I grab my bag and storm from the room.

"Well, she's as delightful as ever." His voice follows me, humour evident in his tone.

I can almost hear David rolling his eyes. "She's always like that. So dramatic. I'd say you'll get used to it, but you never really do."

There's a snort, and Jax says, "Oh, I know. No need to remind me."

My face burns and my eyes prickle, but as I slam into my room I recall the words again: Jax calling me gross, Jax smirking at me, Jax calling me a kid. David's scoff. Jax's snort.

Always the implication that I'm a drama queen, that I'm too much, too emotional, too "out there".

I'm done with them all. I'm done with caring what they all think of me.

And for what he said, Jackson Sherwood will pay.

Chapter Two

JAX

I DUMP the last bag of my clothes onto the floor with the rest of my belongings and survey the room that's mine for the next two months. Or however long it takes me to get my life back together.

I can't believe I've ended up sleeping on a pull-out couch in my best friend's parents' home office.

I also can't believe that in all the years I've known David I had no idea they had this amazing room hidden away. It's off the hallway that leads from the kitchen and living rooms to the garage and laundry room. It's the kind of hallway that doesn't give the impression there's a massive, sunny office on the other side of a door, and I've never paid much attention to what's down here before now.

It's a wide-open space, the couch pushed against one wall with plenty of room for it to be unfolded. A long desk runs along the wall under the window overlooking the backyard. There are cupboards framing each end of the desk and a massive built-in bookshelf covering an entire wall.

I shake my head as I look around in awe. As far as places to end up go, this one isn't so bad. I still wish it hadn't come to this, though.

A month ago I was living in my own place – rented, sure, but I was in charge.

Well, sort of.

I was sharing with four others and I was at the bottom of the food chain, but at least I didn't have parents to contend with and my standards were higher than my flatmates', so I didn't have anyone on my case.

My friend from work, Trent, had got me into the house. His best friend was one of the leaseholders. It was the perfect solution. I could move out of home, leaving Mum to rent her place and finally travel like she's always wanted.

She would have let me stay, probably rent-free, but I know she needs the extra money to fund her trip of a lifetime. I didn't want to take that away from her. And the room I got in the house was way cheaper than what Mum's place could rent for.

But then it all went to hell and here I am, crashing on David's sofa bed until further notice.

David's been my best friend for so many years I can't remember how we met, though Mum tells me it was through school. We ended up on the same childhood sports teams, our mums meeting on the sidelines.

Our friendship was cemented when they came to a mutually beneficial babysitting agreement, sending one of us to the other's house whenever one of them had to work late or cover an extra shift.

It's been a weird year, with him and pretty much all of my other friends away at uni. I'm looking forward to him being back in town for a bit and finally having a chance to catch up on his life.

I flop down onto the sofa bed and cover my eyes with my arm.

What the hell did I do to deserve this strange situation?

Thoughts of Annie start crowding my brain, despite my best efforts to think of something else – anything else.

It's a losing battle. It always is.

I sigh and give up the fight, letting the thoughts swarm in, right as the door bangs loudly.

"What the—"

I jerk upright and almost fall off the edge of the bed.

Essie is standing in the doorway, mouth agape. Her white blouse and green school uniform skirt are gone, along with the knee-high white socks she was wearing when she got home. She's now in denim shorts, the hems frayed, and a turquoise button-down that looks suspiciously like her dad's. She's rolled the sleeves and tied the bottom and looks like a total boss, standing there glaring down at me.

"What are you doing here?" she snipes, her glossy bright pink lips curling into a snarl.

I blink.

I'm used to seeing Essie as sweet, or sarcastically funny; not wicked like she looks now.

"Um, I'm staying here for a bit," I croak, and wonder why I'm cowering at my friend's little sister.

"Here? As in right here in this room? Ugh!" She turns tail and strides from the room without another word.

I flop back onto the bed. At least she's scared away thoughts of Annie.

A raised voice filters down the hallway. Essie's. I wonder who she's yelling at.

I smile to myself. At least it's not me.

Chapter Three

ESSIE

NOT ONLY IS Jax openly mocking me, as per usual, he's taken over the only space in the house I can leave my sewing stuff set up for more than a few hours.

Nobody even told me. They let him move right on into our house and no one said a thing to me.

I almost died of fright when I barged into my parents' office, which I secretly referred to as my studio. Secretly, because to say it aloud would only incite ridicule. And apparently my family have more than enough weaponry in that department.

My parents brushed off my complaints, claiming Jax needed somewhere to stay, and would I prefer that he slept under a bridge somewhere?

No, obviously I wouldn't want that, but he could sleep in David's room, surely.

Except there's been no hint of life from David's room so far today, and I heard Jax's car start up before six, so maybe that's why. Jax actually intends to do something with his life while David intends to sleep the days away.

I slip down the stairs. It's the first day of my summer holidays and the house is quiet. Mum and Dad have both left for work. I assume Jax still has the job he left school halfway through his last year for and that he'll be there all day. It's just me and David.

It's weird having David home again. I've got used to having the house mostly to myself while he's been at uni – studying medical sciences, of all things. Mum and Dad are so proud, only emerging from their own work lives long enough to tell everyone exactly how proud they are. They've been burying themselves in work more and more since I got my driver's licence and no longer need chauffeuring everywhere.

And now David is back and he's everywhere – in the bathroom when I want to use it, moving my stuff in the bathroom, eating food I've saved for myself, usually right in front of me, and always, always floating about with his stupid smug surety that he's so much better than everyone else.

As if that wasn't bad enough, he had to move his best friend in too, so now I have two smug jerks to avoid.

The door is ajar to the office slash studio slash Jax's bedroom, and I sneak inside. I don't know why I'm sneaking, but it feels wrong to be in his space without his knowledge. Even if the space was supposed to be mine for the next two months of the summer holidays so I could sew for days and make a little headway on my stock.

I survey the space. The bed is neatly made, Jax's bags and a few boxes of belongings stacked tidily in the corner. Guess I can't get him kicked out on the grounds of being slovenly.

I sigh and head for the cupboard in the corner where my fabric and notions are stored and start packing them into cardboard boxes.

As I unpack all my supplies and equipment in my room, I simmer.

I stack bundles of fabric in the corner and simmer.

I clear off my desk to set up my sewing machines and simmer.

My room is too small anyway, and packing all of this into it is going to make getting to my bed hazardous. But some part of me refuses to leave it downstairs. I don't want to have to ask Jax's permission to get to my own things. And knowing him, he'd probably lord it over me in some way.

My mind flashes back to last night when I was forced to sit across from him at the dinner table. I recall his smirk when Mum suggested, again, that I get a summer job. Jax has a full-time job and, of course, David already has a holiday job at a restaurant. Mum wasn't telling them to get jobs.

"I have a job," I said, frustration colouring my tone. I've already told her, several times, what I intend to do with my summer. I glanced up then, my eyes locking onto Jax's as the corner of his mouth curled. He looked away the moment my gaze met his, but the smirk remained.

I flop onto my bed, still remembering the look on his face. An unidentifiable emotion, but that curled lip indicated disdain. I can't figure out why, though. What have I ever done to Jax to make him look at me with such distaste every time I'm in the room with him?

My phone rings, interrupting thoughts I don't want to be having.

I grin when I see Brooke's name on the screen and swipe to answer.

"I miss you," she declares before I even have a chance to speak. I laugh and it feels foreign already, even though it hasn't even been twenty-four hours since she left and Jax swarmed into my house.

"I miss you too," I say.

Brooke left yesterday, pretty much the minute school let out for the summer holidays, to stay with her dad for the next few weeks. He lives too far away for her to see him regularly, so they spend as much time together as possible in school holidays.

"Amelia loves her dress," she says, talking about the dress I made for her four-year-old half-sister's birthday. "Tracey's already asked if I can get her one for a wedding they're going to in a couple of months."

I grin. Brooke's my greatest supporter, biggest customer and best advertisement. She buys the children's dresses I make for everyone she knows. "Of course," I say. "Let me know if she wants anything specific and when they need it by."

"I'll email it through as soon as we're done catching up," Brooke says. Then her tone changes. "Speaking of which, you'd better catch me up on your house guest."

I groan. I still can't believe he's here. But I tell her all about my nemesis. "I hate him," I say. "I need to get him to leave."

"I'm sure you're more than capable of making his life so utterly miserable he'll want nothing more than to never set foot in your house again," she says with a laugh. "And I'll help you come up with wicked plans, but for now I have to go."

I sigh. "So do I. This fabric won't cut itself out."

She laughs again, says goodbye and ends the call.

I collect the neatly folded swath of chiffon, my pattern pieces and scissors and head for the only floor space large enough to cope now with my fabric cutting.

Chapter Four

JAX

THE FRONT DOOR is unlocked when I get back to my temporary home after work. I know David isn't here, because he texted me a few minutes ago, already moaning about his summer job.

It's unlikely that it's his parents either, since they both work until 5 and it's only 4.30 now. The pro of starting work early is finishing early too.

But that leaves only one option for who is home right now.

Essie.

She's in the middle of the lounge, kneeling amongst a pile of deep pink fabric that catches the light and sparkles every time she moves it. She doesn't glance up as I walk in, shrugging off my jacket; she just keeps slicing her scissors through the fabric.

I wait until she finishes her cut before speaking. "Hey," I say, wary of her reaction. She seemed so furious yesterday. At me, at the world, I'm not really sure, but it's put me on edge to be around her again, especially without the buffer of David or her parents.

She jerks in surprise and I'm glad I waited until she'd finished cutting before I spoke. She turns her gaze on me, her eyes wide, a hand pressed to her chest.

Her eyes are so green as they take me in. I shift, suddenly awkward, but I can't understand why. I'm not scared she's going to leap across the room and stab me with those scissors clutched in her hand. Maybe I should be, though.

"Hi," she says shortly, then turns away, back to her fabric. She ignores me completely as she finishes cutting out her pieces. She carefully folds them, pinning a small piece of paper to the front of each one, and stacks them in a basket.

I stand and watch her until she places the final piece in the basket and begins to collect the remaining scraps of fabric scattered about the floor. Before she can turn those burning green eyes on me again, I scarper, heading for my own room.

I shut the door behind me and let out a shuddering breath. I don't know what's come over me; what possessed me to stand there for those few minutes and watch her work.

I throw my leather jacket towards the bed and realise something is different about the room. I study the space. None of my things have been touched, nothing moved.

But a box under the desk is gone and a cupboard in the corner is slightly ajar, like it was pushed closed but it didn't go all the way. I haven't looked in the cupboards or opened any drawers. The only things I've allowed myself to examine are the books on the shelf along the wall, because the rest isn't my business.

But I step towards the slightly open cupboard, pulling the door wide to expose the shelves inside, completely bare except for a few stray scraps of fabric and thread.

The entire cupboard is empty and I don't know how much was in here before, but I have a feeling it was a lot.

I step back, shutting the doors and surveying the rest of the room, analysing the size of the space if the sofa bed didn't take up so much of the floor, and realise that there is more than enough room for Essie to have been cutting out that sparkling pink fabric in here.

No wonder she's furious with me. I've kicked her out of her sewing space and no one in her family even told her I was coming, that I was staying.

By the time I make it back to the lounge, there's no sign Essie was ever there.

I climb the stairs, mentally preparing myself for the conversation I want to have. I've got this. I can apologise, tell her to use the space.

I knock on the door to her bedroom, firmly closed against me.

"What?" Essie's voice snaps through the closed door.

I hesitate. I don't know how to answer that. Before I have the chance to think of something to say the door opens, Essie's wild face appearing in the gap. "What do you want?" Those eyes flash.

"I – I didn't realise you used that room," I say eventually.

"Is that it?"

"I didn't know," I say, helplessly. This is not going how I planned, how I imagined.

"Well, now you do. Good for you," she snaps, closing the door in my face.

My agitation spikes. I haven't done anything to this girl. I'm here trying to apologise and she's only been confrontational and angry towards me since I got here.

"Estella!" I shout through the door.

It flies open again and she's there, right in my face. "Don't call me that." I expected her to shriek, to yell and shout and slam the door, but her voice is quiet and lethal. It skitters over my bones as her breath brushes my cheek.

She's that close and the fire in her eyes, the shape of her lips as she speaks, the heaving, shuddering breaths she's taking have stopped me in my tracks, left me speechless.

My eyes meet hers, hold her stare. For moments or minutes or hours we stand there, chest to chest, and breathe, then against my will my gaze drops to her lips, her teeth catching the bottom one between them, and before I even know what's happening my hand is raised between us, reaching for that chewed lip, reaching to free it.

The slightest brush of my thumb against her skin, so slight I'm not even sure if it's real, and Essie whirls away.

She steps back into her room, slamming the door and leaving me in the hallway, knees weak, breath shaking, staring at my hand and wondering what in the hell I've done.

Chapter Five

ESSIE

I LEAN against the door and suck down breaths.

Jax touched my face, brushed his thumb against my lip, like a prelude to kissing me.

Surely not.

Especially not when I remember David telling my parents a couple of months ago that Jax was completely in love with his new girlfriend, Anna or Annabelle or something Anna-ish.

I think he might have come to my room to apologise. There was something in the way he spoke, was so hesitant about being here that makes me think he was sorry.

But he never actually apologised and his conversation with David flashed through my mind again, like it does every time I lay eyes on him. So I shut the door in his face, trying to not let it all bother me and instead think about the dress I'm working on.

My name, though. The way he shouted it through the door, anger sparking in his voice with the word. I couldn't let that go.

And then we were chest to chest, our faces so close I could feel his breath and see the green and gold and brown flecks in his hazel eyes. I was frozen, staring at those eyes, marvelling somewhere in the depths of my mind at how beautiful they were, especially flashing with emotion. He smelled like something kind of burnt. Not burnt food; something else. It should have been repulsive … but it wasn't. I wanted to know what it was.

That touch of his thumb against my lip, so light it almost feels imagined, broke the spell. He touched me, with a girlfriend out there somewhere.

He's so careless. Careless with people's feelings. He's flirted with my friends before, toyed with them with no intention of it ever meaning anything. And not just flirting in passing, not simply being a charming, charismatic person. No, it was more than that. He focused on them, flirting and charming them so consistently until they thought they actually stood a chance of being with him. More than one cried when he turned his attention to the next girl in line. I've seen it time and time again.

The realisation hits me. This is why I'm so furious about that overheard conversation: because Jax flirts with everyone, but not me. Instead, he called me gross, a kid, and joined in on the damning of me as over-dramatic; a word I hate every time someone mentions it.

And then he came to my room and laid that charm on me anyway. I don't know what to think anymore. He's obviously decided I make a fun target. I won't stand for it. My resolve for revenge solidifies as I make my way back to my sewing machine.

Delicious smells make my stomach start rumbling and I

realise it's been two hours since the confrontation with Jax in my bedroom doorway.

I switch off my sewing machine and stretch, my back aching. The initial layers of the chiffon skirt are slowly coming together, but the project is ambitious and I'll never finish it tonight, even if I don't take a break.

So, dinner it is, before Mum starts calling me anyway. Family dinners are pretty much expected in this house, especially since it's usually the only time I see my parents all day.

"Yum, smells good," I say, walking into the kitchen, expecting to see Mum standing beside the stove.

But it's not Mum. It's Jax.

He turns to me, a smile playing on his mouth. I try not to think about his mouth, about how close it was to mine earlier.

"Thanks," he says. "It's nothing fancy—"

I cut him off before he can say more.

"Sorry, thought you were Mum." I grab cutlery and start setting the table, because I'm not letting him show off by cooking while I get told off for not being helpful.

We work in silence for a while but finally he speaks again. I'm filling a glass with water from the excruciatingly slow fridge dispenser when I feel him step close beside me.

"I'm sorry I took over your space. I didn't realise. I'm gone from 6 am until 4.30 every day. You can use it whenever."

"It's fine," I say. "Don't worry."

"Look, Es—"

"No, you look, Jackson," I snarl. "It's fine, use the room. Whatever. I don't care."

He leans against the bench, assessing me coolly. Amusement is playing with his features again. "Your outburst would suggest otherwise, Estella." He drawls out my name and I have never wanted to punch someone in the face so badly.

"Think what you want," I say, trying to level my voice, stop it from shaking. "I still don't care."

He studies me for a moment longer and I force myself to meet his gaze, stare him down. I refuse to blink, to look away.

His eyes flash and he turns away to pull a tray out of the oven.

Chapter Six

JAX

I WALK in the door on Friday night to David and Essie having an almighty brawl.

Well, maybe not a brawl. Essie is standing in the kitchen, hands fisted on her hips, glowering at David, who appears completely nonplussed. She's wearing this swishy black skirt that ends halfway down her thighs and a purple top with huge, puffy sleeves. So many people wouldn't be able to pull it off. They wouldn't even try. On Essie though, it looks awesome. I can't help but smile at her.

"I'm taking the car," Essie is saying. "Mum said I could last week."

David sighs. "Yes, but I need it now, so she's going to take you."

Essie scoffs, "And then' she'll insist on picking me up super early!"

David shrugs. "Not my problem," he says, and turns away.

Essie bristles. She's like a cranky cat preparing to fight off an over-friendly dog. If she had fur it'd be all puffed up.

"Where are you going?" I ask, trying to save my friend from his sister's wrath.

She turns on me, glowering. "Melissa's."

"Melissa McLean?"

She gives a tight little nod. Her mouth, bright pink with glossy lipstick, is pressed in a thin line.

"Jax can take you," David says, turning back to the conversation. He looks at me. "You're going anyway, aren't you?"

I nod. Melissa's my cousin and her older sister Cayley is part of my and David's group of friends. She invited a group of us over to save her from her sister's birthday party.

"Yeah, aren't you?"

David shakes his head. "Got called into work." He pulls a face and I chuckle.

"I can take you," I say to Essie. She studies me, taking in the state of me no doubt, covered in grime and grease. She quirks an eyebrow.

I hold her stare, raise an eyebrow of my own at her. "If you can give me twenty minutes," I say, "Estella." I drag the 's' sound, holding the suspense of which name I'll use, but I can't resist the purse of her lips and shift of her posture at the use of her full name.

She sighs, loud and dramatic. "Fine, Jackson." She does the same thing to my name and I want to smile so badly, but I tamp it down, forcing my features smooth. We stare at each other for another moment before she lets out a huff and turns away.

I grin then, when she can't see, but have to hide it again when David turns to me. "Thanks, man," he says. "And sorry for dumping her on you tonight."

I wave him off. "Don't worry about it. We won't even see each other once we're there."

"Just…" He trails off, but there's a stubborn set to his jaw that tells me he's going to say something and I'm not going to like it. "Don't hit on her, man. It's too weird."

I scoff. "I've already told you. I have no interest in hitting on your sister." I pull a face.

I don't know why he's suddenly so caught up on me hitting on Essie. He's never mentioned it before, and I've known Essie for years as well. I've always thought of her as David's annoying little sister who would pout if we didn't include her in our games. But she used to draw pictures for me, presenting them to me with a flourish every time I came to visit. That hasn't happened for a few years now.

"You'd better not." He turns to leave the room, then spins back to me. "Can you pick up Jeremy too? I told him I'd be his sober driver."

"Yeah, sure," I say. It's not far out of my way and Jeremy is fine, though he's never been a close friend of mine. There's something about him that keeps me at arm's length.

"Thanks, and have fun tonight." David waggles his eyebrows at me. "But not with my sister; she's not your rebound."

I roll my eyes and head for the bathroom, desperate for a shower. I rush through getting ready, trying to block out the thoughts in my head that for once aren't about Annie.

They're about Essie, about the way she looked standing in her bedroom doorway shouting at me, her face inches from mine. They're about the fact that I've always, always liked Essie, annoying little sister or not. I've always thought she was fun, I've always loved her feistiness and I've always thought she was cute. The past few months when I haven't seen her, that cute has evolved, and now all I can think about is the place on her thigh where her skirt ends and the soft curve of the neckline of that purple top she's wearing.

She's still cute, but God help me, now she's also sexy as damn hell. Maybe David's right to be worried.

I shrug my jacket on and walk back to the kitchen. No sign of Essie. She's not in the lounge either. Probably back in her room.

"Yo, Estella!" I call up the stairs. "Time to go."

A moment later she appears at the top of the stairs and although I've already seen her dressed to go out, my stomach flips at the sight of her.

She rushes down the stairs, eyes glued to her phone until she's two steps above me. She freezes, glancing up, eyes meeting mine. They drift down me, widening slightly as they go before locking with mine again.

The step she's on leaves her just a fraction taller than me and my stomach flips again as her perfume hits me. It's sweet and fruity. Edible.

I'm playing a dangerous game. I lift the corner of my mouth into a smirk. "About time. You ready yet?"

She glowers at me.

Yep, I'm playing a *very* dangerous game.

Chapter Seven

ESSIE

WE DRIVE IN SILENCE. There's some rock-type music playing quietly, but other than that and the sounds of the car engine, there's silence between us.

I should probably be more grateful that he offered to drive me, but every time I try to speak no words come out. Also, why should I be pleasant to him, when he spends all his time smirking and glaring at me?

At dinner last night he sat across from me again, a smug little smile on his face creeping wider with every mouthful of lasagne I ate.

Unfortunately it was freaking delicious. So delicious I couldn't even pretend to hate it to spite him. It would have only left me missing out.

Of course, Mum and Dad absolutely gushed over him for cooking dinner. It left me with anger simmering right below the surface, threatening to spill over.

But he did offer to drive me when David was being a total jerk and Mum wasn't home to help argue my point, though she would have probably sided with David anyway.

Jax even cleared off his front seat for me, shifting a huge stack of books and papers into the backseat before I got in. Unfortunately, he followed it up with a huge mocking bow indicating I was free to get in the car, and it made me want to hit him all over again.

I glance towards him and he's looking at me. His gaze flicks away before our eyes really meet, but he was definitely looking at me. I watch him carefully from the corner of my eye, pretending I'm watching out the windscreen, when they flash my way again.

"What?" I snap.

"Nothing," he says, that mouth curling again. I glare at him. "I didn't know you were friends with Melissa," he says casually, as though I'm not trying to kill him with my eyes.

I shrug. "You barely know anything about me, so why would you?"

"I guess," he says, trailing off. He bites his lip, keeping his gaze locked on the street in front of us. No more glances my way.

"What're the books for?" I blurt after a few long moments of silence. I snap my mouth shut, furious at myself for continuing the conversation.

"My course," he says, startled. "I do correspondence for all the theory and work takes care of the practical parts of it."

I can't help it, and the next words are out before I can stop them. At least they're said with some form of disinterest. Wouldn't want him thinking I actually care. "What do you actually do?"

"I'm an engineer," he says. "Well, an apprentice. At the moment I pretty much sweep the workshop but eventually I'll make components for machines, factories and things."

Huh. I study him sidelong, trying to not be obvious about it. Another glance in my direction and he catches me out.

"Is sewing your summer job?" he asks, voice careful.

I sigh. "Yeah, it is, even if no one will believe it's a legitimate job," I say. Words have got to stop coming out of my mouth.

"Do you make money doing it?"

"Yeah," I reply. "I make little things; scrunchies, a few wallets, bags, baby dresses and hats, and sell them at markets. And then sometimes I get asked to make dresses specifically for people."

"Seriously?" Disbelief. Of course.

"Yes, seriously," I snap, my sarcasm biting.

"No, I don't mean it like I don't believe you. That's really cool," he says. "I remember you sewing stuff all the time for your dolls when you were little."

Oh. It might be the least awful thing Jax has ever said to me. I'm left speechless.

Until he turns in the wrong direction. "Uh, Melissa's house is that way," I say, pointing behind us.

He rolls his eyes. "Yes, I am aware. She's my cousin. I know where she lives. We're picking up someone else."

I slump back into my seat, not bothering to reply. His cousin? Melissa has never mentioned Jax is her cousin. I'm not sure I recall her ever mentioning him at all.

I bet it's Jax's girlfriend we're picking up, but I don't ask.

A few minutes later we pull into a driveway and Jax taps the horn. I don't move. There's no way I'm sitting in the back seat, not even for his girlfriend.

But it's not a girl who comes out of the house. It's not a girl who opens the car door and slides into the back seat, cheerfully greeting Jax.

It's a guy. And he's gorgeous.

Chapter Eight

JAX

WE HAD A CONVERSATION.

Exchanged words in a somewhat civil manner.

Essie shuts up fast when Jeremy gets in the car though, and I suddenly wish I hadn't agreed to pick him up. Surely he could have gone without drinking tonight so he could drive himself home?

But I said I'd do an old friend a favour, so here we are. Essie with her phone out, refusing to speak to me anymore. I ignore the little pang in my chest.

Jeremy asks how I've been, asks how the job's going, all the while flicking eyes towards Essie.

"Jeremy," I say, getting the introductions out of the way. "This is David's little sister, Es—" Her head twists towards me, staring me down, as if daring me to call her Estella. Not even I'm that brave. "—sie." I finish, firing her a little smile as she turns away. "Essie, Jeremy."

"Hey," she mumbles in response to his greeting.

"You on holidays now?" he asks.

"Yeah." Another mumble.

"Summer job?"

"Um, not re—"

I cut her off. Not really? As if. "Essie's got her own business," I say, ignoring the glare she's sending my way.

"Oh yeah? What do you do?" Jeremy asks.

"I sew a bunch of things and sell them at markets. And make custom dresses," she says. Her tone is different than when she told me, but I can't figure out why. It's almost like she's playing this off as not a big deal. It makes me a little angry.

I park just down the street from Cayley and Melissa's house and by the time I'm standing on the footpath, Jeremy has already fallen into step with Essie – who was out of the car in a flash – continuing their conversation by peppering her with questions as we walk.

I trail along behind, trying to find an opening where I can butt in, so I can let her know we can go whenever she wants to. But I don't get the chance. We reach the house and she disappears inside without so much as a glance at me.

I follow Jeremy to the kitchen where Cayley is dumping chips into a bowl.

"Hello!" She grins when she sees us. She tosses the chip bag away and picks up the bowl, along with a plate of pizza slices.

"Need a hand?" I ask.

"God, yes please," Cayley says, nodding towards a stack of bottles in the corner of the bench. "Can you grab some of those?"

I give her a nod then collect as many of the bottles as I can. Coke, Sprite, orange juice, probably to be used as mixers with vodka or whatever other hard liquor this bunch of teens have got their hands on. There must be some of them who are already eighteen. I wonder if I'm supposed to keep an eye on Essie; if she has rules she's supposed to be following, aside from her curfew. I assume it's the same as David's always was, though I'm pretty sure none of this is my problem.

I stop in the doorway between the kitchen and the deck that spans the back of Cayley's house. String lights wind their way along the deck railings and up the verandah posts. A brazier is burning down on the lawn, and it leaves the whole area bathed in a golden glow. A speaker is thumping and there are teenagers milling about everywhere. There's lots of people here, most congregating on the lawn in small clusters.

But I spot Essie immediately. Her dark hair falls down her back as she tips her head back and laughs.

Gone is the angry, confrontational girl. The girl with a glare and acid tongue that could fell grown men. Here, with her friends, she's totally different.

She's grinning now, another girl slipping her arm around her waist and leaning in to speak to her over the music.

"Dude, you're in the way," Jeremy says behind me and I startle, stepping forward and out of the doorway. I don't know how long I've been standing there, transfixed, but however long it was, even if it was barely a second, it's way, way too long to be looking at Essie like that.

I stand the drinks on the table Cayley points to, then retreat to the corner of the deck, where the outdoor furniture has been reserved for us. Jeremy has vanished down the steps onto the lawn and into the party.

"No teenage brats allowed," Cayley declares, and I laugh.

"Cay, you're a teenager still, you know."

"Yes," she says, lifting her chin, "but I'm no brat."

"Keep telling yourself that," I say, collapsing onto the cushions. Cayley grins at me. "No Andrew tonight?" I look around for her boyfriend but he's nowhere in sight.

"Nah." She shakes her head and pulls a sad puppy face. "He's visiting his mum for a while. I miss him already, but he had to go," she says, forcing away the sad expression with a tight smile, and holds out a beer.

I shake my head. "Driving."

She nods and gestures to the selection of drinks I've carried out, and when I shake my head she pops the top off the beer, falling down beside me. "Did you come with Essie?"

I nod. "I'm staying at David's. She needed a ride."

Cayley's face changes in an instant. The smile drops, her eyes go wide, mouth soft. "Oh, I heard. I'm sorry."

I try to smile. "It's all good, Cay. Apparently it's for the best."

She gives me a playful shove. "Come on, it's not like you've ever had trouble with girls. You'll be fine."

I snort. "I quite liked that particular one, though."

She raises her bottle in silent agreement and we fall into silence.

Thoughts of Annie swarm me; her pale gold hair and the way it felt when I'd run my fingers through it, the way she fit perfectly under my arm, her body tucked in close to mine.

Cayley is right. Girls have never been a problem for me. I've dated my fair share, but none seriously. Usually we were simply having a good time for a short time, and I was upfront with them the whole way along. Unfortunately, the girls didn't always take it that way, and somewhere along the line I picked up this reputation as a heartbreaker. I guess it's not entirely unfounded.

Annie was different from the other girls, though. I wanted to be different with her.

We dated for six months and I was convinced I was in love with the sweetest person in the world.

Until she wasn't so sweet anymore and I wondered if I understood anything at all about love.

"I've always liked Essie, you know," Cayley says, scattering my thoughts and bringing me back to the present. "Of all my sister's friends, I like her the most, by far." I raise an eyebrow, wondering where Cayley is going with this. "She's so bold. I'm a little envious of her, actually."

"Envious?" Now I'm curious.

"Yeah, she's so strongly her own person. She doesn't blend in with the crowd, and she's wickedly sarcastic and funny."

I snort a little. "Yeah, it's so funny when she absolutely hates your guts," I say.

"She hates you? Why? What'd you do?"

I laugh at Cayley's assumption it's entirely my fault. "Yeah. And I have no idea. I exist? I'm staying in her house?"

"Maybe she's mean to you because she likes you?" Cayley teases, giving me a wink.

"Cay, girls aren't mean to you if they like you. That's outdated and toxic. She plain hates me. It's that simple." I brush it off with a laugh, but it feels hollow.

Why am I suddenly so concerned about Essie's feelings towards me?

Chapter Nine

ESSIE

MUSIC IS THRUMMING through my bones, lights swirling in my eyes. I'm surrounded by light and laughter as I relax into the beat.

Getting here has left me wound tight. I didn't even realise until the feeling eased, once I was surrounded by music and my friends were there.

Losing the car to David probably set it off. The abrupt change in plans, the fight with him, having to ask Jax for help. I like to be in control. I like the ability to leave whenever I want and not have to ask Jax to drive me home.

But we did almost have a conversation, and it wasn't completely awful. In fact, it was kind of nice. Especially when he told Jeremy about my business. I've always called it that, but most other people don't. Most people call it a waste of time.

Not Jax though, and apparently not Jeremy either, who continued asking me questions about it as we walked into the party. He smiled at me right outside the front door, leaned in close and said he'd see me later, then gestured for me to go in first.

With every question he asked, the flittering sensation in my chest grew, but something settled inside me too.

Jeremy didn't need to be speaking to me. He could have ignored me and spoken only to Jax, but he didn't. Jeremy wanted to talk to me. I hold on to that thought, remember the brush of his fingers against my elbow as he leaned in, the touch of his breath on my cheek.

It all distracted me enough that I forgot to be nervous about being with friends I'm still finding my feet around.

I've been friends with Brooke since we started high school and I was dumped in a class with none of my old friends. Things with Brooke are easy. I know where I stand. But over the past few months she's started introducing me to other friends, bringing them over to hang out with us, or arranging for us to spend time with them, and I still haven't figured out where I fit into the new dynamic.

They're all super kind and hilarious, and have been more than welcoming to me, but for some reason I still can't trust it. I keep waiting for them to realise who I truly am and drop me like a rock.

But, of course, my fears were again unfounded. Melissa hugged me the minute she laid eyes on me. The book and chocolate I gave her for her birthday got me another hug. She tugged me down the steps from the deck to the lawn and into the crowd. Within moments I was surrounded by friends, falling into easy conversation, laughing and understanding their secret inside jokes because I was on the inside.

Now we're dancing.

Sara grabs my hand, twirling me, and we stumble a little, giggling. I've had a couple of drinks tonight, which I don't normally do because I'm always driving, and it's left me tipsy and silly.

A hand lands on my waist, another on my shoulder, and I look up, expecting to see one of my friends.

I suck in a breath. It's not one of my friends. It's Jeremy, his big, warm hands steadying me. Sara, Melissa, the noise and lights of the party all fade into the background.

"Careful," Jeremy says, leaning down to speak into my ear, to be heard over the noise. I shiver as his breath touches my cheek. "You okay?"

I nod, my mouth forming a smile. "I'm good," I say.

He steps closer. So close. He moves, dancing. Both his hands are on my waist now, holding me against him, but lightly. I could easily step away.

But I don't.

I don't want to. The heat and pressure of him against me makes my stomach flip and twist, but in an entirely different way to the nerves I was experiencing earlier.

"You're gorgeous," Jeremy says against my cheek.

My eyes flutter closed at his words, but I force myself to open them, to look up into his face. "Not so bad yourself," I say, voice shaking, hoping he can hear me above the noise.

He grins. He heard me.

We dance, sometimes close, sometimes drifting apart, but even if our bodies aren't touching, Jeremy keeps his eyes on me. Occasionally my friends tear me away, pulling me into their circles, and Jeremy always lets me go, even if I don't want him to because I don't want him to be gone when I look up.

But he never is. He stays, and so I dance with my friends too, losing myself in the music and chaos and brush of Jeremy's hands against me.

Eventually, after what feels like eternity, I tire. My feet ache and my throat is dry. Sweat has gathered along my hairline but I'm grinning like a fool. I make it to the edge of the mass of people, finding a wooden seat that I know is the perfect afternoon hangout, shaded by the gorgeous tree overhead.

I fall onto it and glance up when a pair of denim-clad legs appear beside me.

"Drink?" Jeremy asks.

"Please," I reply, smiling up at him. "Water or Coke or something," I say, but he's already disappearing into the crowd.

By the time he returns my breathing has returned to normal and I'm beginning to cool down.

He slides onto the seat beside me and hands me a vodka RTD. I glance at it then back at him as he takes a swig of beer. "Okay?" he asks, glancing at me, then the drink. "Oh, did you not want that?" He reaches for it as if to take it back. "I'm sorry, I'll go swap it for something else."

"No," I say, "no, it's okay. This is fine." I twist the top off, bring the bottle to my lips and take a sip. The fizz dances over my tongue. He mustn't have heard me ask for something that wasn't alcohol. It wasn't his fault and it doesn't really matter.

Jeremy's arm slides along the top of the seat behind me as he inches closer. I shiver.

"You cold?" he asks, and I nod.

"Just a little," I say, "now that I've stopped dancing."

He grins. "You were doing a lot of that."

Each word brings him closer, until my vision is wholly captivated by his blue eyes. His arm wraps around me, pulling me into him, and I let myself lean in, savouring the warmth of his body.

He's murmuring something. I can't really hear but I get the gist of what he's saying from his body. His other hand comes up to lift my chin, tilting it perfectly for when his lips land on mine.

Chapter Ten

JAX

CAYLEY BEGS ME TO DANCE.

I refuse. She pouts and dances by herself while I protect our seats and catch up with other friends as they drop in and out – some staying for a while, others passing in a blur as they flit about the party.

No one mentions Annie and I only catch a couple of sorrowful looks cast in my direction.

A couple of girls hang around in the periphery, giggling and sending me looks that are far more hopeful than sorrowful. Because apparently, even though I'm a heartbreaker who refuses to stick around, they're interested? I don't understand it. Maybe they think they'll be the ones to make me want to change my mind and become a respectable boyfriend.

Annie was that girl, and look what happened there. Not even she took me seriously, or believed I could do it, or thought I was worth it.

I nurse a plastic cup of Coke, then go drinkless, all because I can't be bothered getting up and walking a couple of metres.

Jeremy saunters past at one point, snagging a beer and something else, saluting me with them before heading back into the crowd.

Fatigue has hit me and when I glance at my phone I realise why. It's after midnight. I haven't seen Essie in hours; just a flash of her here and there through the crowd, which is slowly thinning. I worry about driving home. I'm going to ruin Jeremy's vibe if I leave now, but I care far less about that than I do about Essie's reaction. Though I suspect she has a 1 am curfew, so we'd better get moving whether she wants to or not. I push out of my seat, taking a deep breath before I descend the steps into the throngs of the party. A few are still dancing, including Melissa and Cayley. I admire their commitment.

I scan the last few dancers. No sign of Essie. I sigh. I have to start hunting shadowy corners for her. Hopefully I'll find Jeremy on the way, because I do not want to contemplate the shadowy corners I might find him in.

Under the tree Cayley and I used to climb as kids I catch a flash of purple, a bare, tanned leg and a tumble of dark hair.

Found her.

I stop dead when I realise she's wrapped around someone. There's a twist somewhere low in my gut but I ignore it. I cannot trust my feelings at the moment.

I can't make out who it is in the dimness. Even though he's sitting on an old wooden seat, I can tell he's tall. He's towering over her and his hand is gliding along her thigh. I tense when it disappears under the edge of her skirt.

But Essie's hand drops from the guy's shoulder to his hand and she gently pushes it back down her leg. I can breathe again.

I'm standing here gawking and it's creepy and weird, but we really do need to leave soon.

I'm still standing there, staring, when his hand moves on her thigh again. Even from this distance I can see Essie stiffen.

She pushes his hand away again. They break off kissing for him to say something to her and when she turns her head to smile at him and say something back, I realise who it is.

Jeremy.

And the bastard has just put his hand back on her leg. On top of her skirt, but close enough to the edge that she's still uncomfortable.

"Essie," I say, approaching them. "We need to go."

They pull apart again and she glances up at me, her eyes wide, lips parted. Jeremy's hand on her thigh.

"Not yet," she says.

"We need to go or you'll miss curfew," I say, and she scowls.

"She's got plenty of time," Jeremy says, words slurring together, and I watch his fingers tighten. Essie stiffens again and I want to punch him.

"She really doesn't. Come on, Essie." My voice is firm, but I'm keeping it calm. Now is not the time to trigger one of her tempers.

Jeremy stands, slightly unsteady. He pulls Essie up beside him and I catch the moment when his hand slips under her skirt again.

I want to break all his fingers.

Essie's eyes flash for a second then her posture changes, eyes dropping and arms crossing over her chest, but not in the defiance I usually see from her.

"Come on, Ess," he says to her. "We can continue this on the way home."

"Dude," I say to my friend. "I'm leaving now. Essie is coming with me. What you do with the rest of your night is up to you, but find a new way home."

Jeremy murmurs something to her that I can't hear, and it makes her mouth tilt up again. Her crossed arms loosen, the uncomfortable posture melting away again.

"You can't leave him here," Essie says, glowering at me again.

"I can and I am," I say. "He's a big boy. Now, come on Essie."

Jeremy sneers at my tone. He turns to Essie, voice low enough that I can't hear. They whisper for a few moments, trading stupid smiles and a few brief kisses.

I lose patience. "Estella," I snap, and she turns to me.

"Fine." She turns back to Jeremy, squeezes him in a hug, whispering something in his ear, and lets go. She storms past me, shoving into me as she goes. I shoot Jeremy a final glare and follow her.

She's on the street before I catch up to her and when I do she spins to face me. "How dare you!" she shouts.

"I was looking out for you," I say, trying to keep my voice calm, but it's shaky and on edge.

"I don't need you to look out for me. I'm not some damsel in distress who needs you to swoop in and save me."

"I know you're not," I say, taking deep breaths. "But I could see you were uncomfortable. You asked him to stop and he didn't."

Her face goes red, cheeks flushing with embarrassment or anger or something else. I don't know.

"He just got caught up in the moment," she says with a little huff. "He didn't realise where his hands were. He was stopping." But she's crossed her arms again like she's uncertain of what she's saying.

"Believe me when I say a guy would have a very, very good idea of where his hands are on a girl's body." My voice comes out low and rough.

"Yeah, well you'd know, wouldn't you," she snaps, and my insides recoil at not only the words but also the poison in them.

"You were uncomfortable and he wasn't stopping. I was looking out for you," I say through my teeth, not letting her see how hard her interruption hit me.

"I can look out for myself." She's glowering at me again, arms dropping to her sides and forming fists. "I'll prove it. Put your hands on me and I'll show you what I'd do to a guy who touches me when I don't want to be." She steps in close, eyes locking with mine. Her fury is palpable.

I lean in, keeping my arms tight against my sides. "I'm not going to put my hands on you, Estella," I say, my voice a low growl, "not unless I'm one hundred percent sure that you want me to." The words are out before I have a chance to think about them, to censor them, and once they're out in the world I realise the meaning behind them.

Her eyes go wide as she takes in what I've said and she sucks in a shaky breath. We're so close again, almost nose to nose in the street, breathing each other's air. I catch a whiff of that delicious perfume she wears. She shouldn't go around smelling so edible.

I'm consumed by the desire to touch her, to swipe away the smudge of makeup under her eye, to brush back the stray strands of hair stuck to her flushed cheek. To do all sorts of things I just swore I wouldn't.

But I won't touch her – not now, not ever – unless she wants me to. I stride past her, carefully avoiding contact as I realise exactly how much I want to.

"Get in the car. We're going home."

Chapter Eleven

ESSIE

I'M NOT GOING *to put my hands on you, Estella, not unless I'm one hundred percent sure that you want me to.*

I replay the words over and over as we sit in awkward, angry silence on the drive home.

Does that mean he wants to? He wants to touch me?

I flick my eyes his way, spying him out of the corner of my eye, afraid to actually turn my head to look. His hands are clenched around the steering wheel, knuckles looking like they're about to burst, and there's a tense line that runs through him, from the death grip on the wheel to the set of his jaw and straightness of his back.

I replay his words again. How different they are to what he said to my brother only a few days ago, when he called me a kid and implied I was gross.

I've held onto those words. Jax's opinion of me shouldn't matter. I shouldn't care. But for some reason I haven't been able to let it go. Maybe it's because once upon a time I really liked Jax. I thought he was funny, and when David was mean to me, Jax never was.

...unless I'm one hundred percent sure that you want me to.

My stomach flip flops and my heart thunders when I think of what it might mean. It makes me nauseous.

But it's preferable to thinking about what else happened tonight. It's definitely preferable to wondering if Jax is right about Jeremy, if he was fully aware of what he was doing.

I knew for every second of our encounter where my hands were, because they felt like they were on fire every time I touched him. I knew where his hands were too – especially when one landed on my thigh, because that one felt cold. Not his actual hand. His hand was warm and large and gentle and everything I expected it to be, but the feeling of it against the bare skin of my leg sent a cold shiver through me.

So I pushed him away, and then again. I was feeling uncomfortable, and when we stood and he slid his hand up the back of my thigh, pressing his hand against my ass for a brief second, I flared with anger.

But it didn't feel worth the scene I'd cause to object, and then he whispered apologies about getting caught up in the moment and sweet compliments that made me want to curl into him again, to have that smooth voice murmuring in my ear, telling me that I was beautiful, gorgeous, sexy as hell.

For a moment I was sick of being the girl who always stood out, who caused drama, who always had to shove her opinion out into the world. I didn't want to cause a scene or be dramatic or fight with Jeremy. What he did was harmless; a compliment, really. Wasn't it?

But Jax ruined the whole thing anyway. He stormed in, glowering at us with his hands on his hips, and embarrassed me like I've never been before in my life. David's kid sister, that's all he thinks of me as, despite the way he spoke afterwards, about putting his hands on my body.

I shiver as I recall the way my name rolled off his tongue – utterly furious and also something else – and the way his eyes went dark in the seconds following the words.

It's not a shiver that makes me feel cold, though. I don't feel cold until I remember the way he stalked past me, keeping an obvious distance between us, and told me to get in the car.

We pull into the driveway and Jax puts the car in park, turning the engine off.

"Este— Essie," he says, and for a second I miss the way he emphasises the 'a' on the end of Estella.

I don't bother to look at him. I'm not sure what I'd see, or how I'd feel. Instead, I push open the door, place one foot on the concrete and climb out of the car.

"I'm sorry, Essie," he says, his voice soft as I slam the door and head inside, locking myself in my room where the tears begin to fall.

Tears of embarrassment, and shame, and something like sadness, which I can't quite figure out, because they're all tangled up with thoughts of Jax and how he sits in the car for long, silent minutes after I've left, and that doesn't make sense at all.

I wake early the next morning to my phone buzzing on the table beside my bed. I groan, rolling over to pick it up.

Brooke.

I swipe to answer and her voice fills my ear before I even have the chance to say hello.

"Tell me everything," she says, voice gushing.

"About what?" I say groggily, pushing myself upright then settling back against the headboard.

"Melissa told me you spent quite a lot of time last night with a guy she didn't know so assumed was one of Cayley's friends."

Oh. I haven't really considered this. That people will have seen us together, that I'll have to tell them what happened.

How am I going to do that when I'm not even sure what happened? With Jax interrupting us we didn't have a chance to talk about anything, or for me to give him my phone number. That's assuming he wanted my phone number.

"Was it Jax?" Brooke asks, intruding on my thoughts and bringing me back to the conversation.

I laugh. "Well, Jax is Melissa's cousin, so I'd hope she knows who he is."

"Jax is her cousin? She's never said."

"Maybe she doesn't want to be associated with him in any way. A wise move if you ask me." My tone is bitter, matching my cranky feelings towards Jax. I was wondering what they'd be like this morning. I guess I have the answer.

Brooke laughs. The sound is too loud and bright for the number of hours of sleep I've had.

"No, it was definitely not Jax. His name is Jeremy and he's a friend of Cayley and Jax. We only danced a bit …" I trail off, remembering last night: Jeremy's smile, his heavy-lidded eyes as he murmured along my cheek, the press of his lips against mine.

"And?"

"And there was perhaps some kissing." I feel the heat race to my face, relieved this is a phone conversation.

"Oooh la la," Brooke squeals, and I pull the phone away from my ear to save my eardrum. "Then what happened? Are you dating him? Please tell me you're seeing him again?"

I scowl, the heat in my cheeks vanishing. "I have no idea," I say, bitterness clogging my voice.

"What? Why?"

"Jax is why," I bite out. "The bastard interrupted us, then insisted I was leaving because he was my ride and therefore responsible for getting me home. And then he pretty much told me that Jeremy was using me for a good time. Not that it's any of his business."

"He did not!" Brooke gasps, her voice verging on ridiculous in its indignation.

"He did." I sigh and slump down in the bed again. "It was mortifying," I whimper to my friend.

"All the more reason to get moving on those wicked plans to get him to never want to set foot near you again," she says. "I highly suggest destruction via seduction … then when you've got him on the hook, gut him."

I burst out laughing at the suggestion and the wickedness in her voice.

"Go on," she says. "Do it."

Chapter Twelve

JAX

THERE'S an aggressive amount of banging coming from behind the wall, like someone is throwing things against it.

Essie, likely. With the way she glared at me all day yesterday, or ignored me completely, I doubt she'd be concerned about the fact she was rearranging the cupboard that shares a wall with where I put my head to sleep.

She didn't speak a single word to me yesterday. Not a peep. There wasn't a snarl or a snipe. She didn't even bite my head off when I asked her to pass the broccoli at the dinner table.

I shove myself out of bed, glancing at the glowing numbers of the clock on the desk.

"What the hell, Estella?" I say, flinging the door of my temporary bedroom open. She's still rummaging in the cupboard but pulls her head out long enough to throw a disdainful glare in my direction before disappearing again. "It's six o'clock on a Sunday. I'm trying to sleep." My voice is low and dark. I sound like a cranky brat, but seriously, I'm up early every other day of the week. I didn't sleep Friday night after the party and barely last night. I was too tangled up with thoughts of Essie, of Jeremy's hands on her and how I'd ever get her to not hate me so vehemently.

She steps out of the cupboard again and shoves it closed. "So sorry to disturb your precious sleep, but some of us have places to be."

"So go be there, instead of banging against the wall at some ridiculous time of the morning."

"I would be long gone," she says, anger flaring in her eyes, and dammit, my heart flips – "except Mum's car won't start and my useless brother lost the jumper leads."

"They're in the other car," I say automatically, immediately recalling I saw them in there last weekend when we went to the beach.

Essie slams her hand against the wall and lets out a sound that's a cross between a shriek and a growl. She pulls her hand back immediately, pressing the palm against her chest like it really hurt.

"Where are you going, anyway?" I ask, and she drops her hand, shaking it out like she can't show fear or pain in my presence. I study her as she eyes me suspiciously. She's fully dressed in a really cute emerald green skirt and white top. A pink cardigan hugs her arms and her hair is pulled up into two messy buns, one on each side of her head. Her makeup is more subtle than Friday night when it was all dark, moody eyes and bright pink lips, but she's still obviously wearing it. At 6 am on a Sunday.

She glares at me some more, then sighs. "I was supposed to be at a market. But it's not like I can walk there." Her eyes close, the dim morning light picking up the gold shimmer on her eyelids, and she tips her head back, muttering something to the heavens.

"I can drive you," I say, surprising even myself.

Her chin returns to its natural level, which for Essie is an inch or two above where most people carry their chins because she is fierce about the world. It makes me want to smile but I manage to resist.

I know it had been a few months since I'd seen her before I moved in here, but I don't remember her being this … whatever she is. I haven't managed to find the right word for it yet.

Yes, she's dramatic, and over the top, and defiant and fiery, but none of those seem like the slurs I've heard David use them as.

"Why?" she asks, pulling me from my thoughts.

"What do you mean, why?"

"Exactly that. Why?"

"Because you need to be somewhere and your car won't start and how else are you going to get there?" She says nothing. I take a deep breath and fight my rising frustration at her stubbornness. "If I don't drive you, can you still go?"

She bites her bottom lip, dragging the glossy pink curve between her teeth. Eventually she looks away. "No," she mutters.

"Do you need to go?" I ask. I'm pretty sure this market is a big deal for her. It's a massive, pre-Christmas one. Vendors and customers come from all over the place to buy handmade and unique Christmas presents. I know nothing about markets, but even I've heard of it, and I assume her not being able to go would leave a big chunk missing from whatever money she was anticipating making this summer.

"Yes," she mutters again, still unable to meet my eyes.

"Estella," I say, and her gaze finally finds mine. She looks defeated; more defeated than I've ever seen her. "Come on." I take a step towards her. "Let's put your stuff in my car. I'll drive you."

Her eyes drop and I realise we've had this whole conversation with me standing shirtless in the hallway. It's a good thing I've taken to wearing actual pyjama pants to sleep in while staying in someone else's house. Essie's eyes widen slightly and her teeth release her lip. I want to run my thumb along it.

We stand there staring at each other for far too long.

Then she presses her lips together, eyes flashing back up to mine. "I was supposed to leave ten minutes ago," she says.

"You start loading your stuff. My keys are on the hook. I only need five minutes."

Her eyes drop below my chin again, lingering for a moment before she turns on her heel. "For the love of God, please remember a shirt," she flings over her shoulder as she strides away.

Chapter Thirteen

ESSIE

I'M EXPERIENCING another silent car ride with Jax.

How has this become my life?

I'd unloaded everything out of my car – well, my parents' car – and was trying to figure out how to drop Jax's back seats so I could fit it all in his car when he appeared, still shoving his feet into shoes.

He looked a little dishevelled, his brown hair tousled, but at least he was wearing a shirt now. The image of him standing in the hallway in just a pair of dark blue pyjama pants sitting low on his hips flashed through my mind as he stepped up beside me, waiting for me to move, then lowered the seats with a few simple movements.

The image flashes through my mind again now as I sit in the car, resolutely staring out the window, refusing to look in Jax's direction.

He tried talking to me but gave up when I refused to engage, and is now singing along quietly to the radio, tapping his fingers against the steering wheel.

I can't really deny it anymore.

Jax is hot.

I've always managed to detach myself from it before. Like, I know he's attractive, with that stupidly cute, floppy brown hair and hazel eyes and freckles across his nose. Even his annoying grin that makes me want to throw things at his head because I know he's mocking me with it is adorable and gorgeous and charming … and so, so stupid.

But I've always been slightly removed from feeling anything about his looks.

Until Friday night when he shouted at me and said those words that made me think he wanted to touch me. Touch me in ways one shouldn't want to touch one's best friend's gross kid sister.

And then he stood there in only pyjama pants, still sleep-rumpled, and my stomach bottomed out.

Brooke suggested I use my feminine wiles to destroy him. To reel him in with flirtation and seduction, then exact my revenge for the embarrassment and shame he's caused me.

And I thought about it.

But when I walked into the kitchen yesterday morning to see him sitting at the table surrounded by textbooks I nearly tripped over my own feet, and every time I opened my mouth to say something both saucy and scalding to him, no words came out. So seduction seems out of my scope.

And now I have the bigger problem that he is helping me; really, really helping me out, and it feels really awful to still want to destroy the guy who is currently driving me across town to go to this market.

I've been preparing for weeks, sewing non-stop, showcasing what I'll have available on my social media, building up a following.

I need today. I need the money from today to buy more fabric to get me through the rest of my summer sewing. My funds are severely depleted after buying the raspberry-pink chiffon for a completely unnecessary dress. It's not like I have anywhere to wear the thing, but the design lodged in my head and wouldn't let go.

This market is a huge event and it's already bustling with vendors when Jax pulls in the gate. I hand over my registration details and the person on the gate guides us to where I'll be setting up.

"You're just in time," she says with a kind smile. "Gates will be closing to traffic soon."

I'm running so late because of that stupid car and David having the jumper leads, which would have been fine – if he'd come home last night.

Jax parks at my stall location and climbs out of the car, immediately starting to unload my tables and gazebo, boxes of stock and other bits and pieces I need for my set up.

"Thanks," I say, my tone abrupt. "You don't need to stay, though. I'll get someone to pick me up this afternoon."

He eyes me as I struggle to extract the gazebo from its bag, then steps in and with an eye roll silently lifts it, making it easy for me to drag the bag away. With his help the gazebo is up in seconds, saving me from the lengthy, exhausting process I normally have to go through alone.

In efficient movements he has tables set up. I try not to stare at the way his arms move and flex as he deftly sets up my stall for me.

"What goes where?" he finally asks, gesturing to my boxes of stock.

"If you don't go now, you'll be stuck here all day," I say, my voice coming out somewhat more aggressively than intended.

He flattens his hand on the table between us, leaning over. "Estella, this market starts in ten minutes. You're not ready. Let me help."

I meet his stare, trying to ignore the heat in my face as my name rolls off his tongue. I know he's still mocking me with it, taunting me with the name I don't let anyone call me. But the way the last syllable curls into my stomach every time he says it, I can't fight him on it anymore.

"Fine," I say, "but you can't say I didn't warn you. That box needs to be put out on that table." I gesture to the box of dresses. "Try to keep the sizes together. There's a couple on hangers that go up there." I gesture towards the framing of the gazebo.

He nods, turning away, and I avert my gaze as he bends down to the box. I do *not* need that kind of distraction today.

I start unpacking my other boxes, stacking headbands and scrunchies into their little baskets and setting up my cash box and the portable eftpos machine that links to my phone and costs me more money than anything else in this business.

"They don't all fit," Jax says, standing over the still-half-full box and looking lost as he stares down at the table.

I step closer to him so I can see how he's laid them out, which is exactly how I usually do it, except somehow it looks better. "Yeah, they're to fill in the gaps as I sell things." I close the lid of the box and move to lift it.

"Here," he says, taking the box before I can get hold of it.

I scowl. "I don't need you to carry the heavy things for me, Jax," I say. "I'm quite capable."

"I know you are, Estella, but you've got customers to deal with."

I turn around and he's right. A young woman with a baby strapped to her chest is rummaging in the basket of scrunchies.

I push thoughts of Jax – and his biceps flexing as he lifted the box and all the things he makes me feel – away as I plaster on my best customer service smile and take my place behind my table.

Chapter Fourteen

JAX

ESSIE IS ... positively sparkling.

She brought a foldable chair with her array of market paraphernalia but she hasn't had a chance to use it, so I've taken to lounging on it at the edge of the stall.

I should have left, because why would I want to spend the whole day at this market? But we arrived so late, and Essie was frantic. I couldn't leave her with boxes of stuff to lay out and a huge great gazebo, which I assume she sets up on her own every other time.

By the time we were done the gates were closed to traffic so my car was stuck here until the end, and Essie had her first customer.

She lit up speaking to that woman in a way she's never spoken to me, and it left a little pain in my chest. It's the sort of pain I used to get thinking about Annie, who I realise hasn't crossed my mind for a couple of days. I can't actually remember when I last thought of her, but definitely not since Friday night when Essie wore that stupid purple top with the puffy sleeves and made me furious with jealousy when I found her making out with Jeremy.

Jeremy, of all people. Sure, he's my friend, or he was once upon a time, and a nice enough guy, but does he really have anything going for him? Do girls find that over-styled blond hair attractive? Is it that he's uber-tall? I can't figure it out.

I also can't figure out how I've ended up in a situation where I am wildly jealous of someone else for getting to make out with Essie. That's a whole other thing to ponder, but I'm refusing to let myself consider it too much right now.

Essie's chatting with her latest bunch of customers. They're talking about some detailing on one of the baby dresses I set out on the tables this morning. I'm still waiting for Essie to rearrange the whole table, but she hadn't changed anything about my layout. I might have even caught the corner of her mouth tilting upwards at the sight of it. I'm trying not to let that teeniest of smiles go to my head.

"No, I can do customs," Essie is saying to an older woman.

"Oh, that would be wonderful, dear. I want matching ones for all my granddaughters."

Essie's smile splits her face as she speaks further with the woman, taking details of the order.

How on earth can her parents not think this is a viable job? She's not even eighteen and has these people falling over themselves to buy her items.

Speaking of which, more baby dresses are sold, leaving gaps in the table, and before Essie has a chance to restock more customers move in.

I push myself out of the chair, reaching into her neatly organised box of surplus stock, and fill the gaps, trying for a range of fabrics and sizes to showcase everything she has to offer.

She turns back in my direction as I carefully arrange the final dress and I think she might be looking at me with gratitude. I shoot her a little smile and step out of the way as a blonde woman reaches towards the table.

I slide behind Essie, careful not to touch her because dammit, I'm keeping my promise, even as my hands itch to trail along her lower back, yearn for the feel of her pressing into my hands.

"Coffee?" I murmur softly, so I don't distract her too much from all the customers vying for her attention. She nods her head slightly and I disappear into the crowds, not able to take a full breath until she's vanished from sight behind me.

I find a coffee cart and join the end of the line. I'm fourth from the front when it suddenly occurs to me that I have no idea how Essie likes her coffee. She put milk in one yesterday morning, but I don't ever remember seeing her put sugar in it and I am entirely clueless as to which of the barista versions she likes.

I drag my phone out of my pocket and pull up Instagram, searching for her account. Surely she's got an account. I find one with her face as the profile picture, but it's private. Rats. In her bio, though, is another account. One for Starlight Stitches. Her business page. I tap, and the feed is filled with bright colours; shots of the baby dresses and market items interspersed with photos of Essie in colourful outfits.

There's a photo from Friday night, taken in her bedroom, that purple top sliding down her shoulder, a wide smile on her face. The caption is details of the top, telling us the fabric it's made from and that she self-drafted the pattern, which I guess means she made it up herself. My brain glitches as I try to figure out how that's even possible.

It does explain why I never see other girls wearing clothes quite like hers, though. She makes them all herself. Well, a lot of them, anyway. I tear myself away from staring at the photo for any longer as the coffee line inches forward. I scroll her feed frantically, but there isn't a single photo of coffee that might give me clues.

"Hey," the girl says to me as I step to the front of the line, still trying to come up with an order. "What can I get for you?" She smiles and I barely register.

"Um, can I grab a cappuccino, and um …" I drop my voice, eyes ranging over the menu. "Essie, Essie," I mutter.

"Oh, are you ordering for Starlight Essie?" the girl asks, and I turn my gaze on her. She's wearing a scrunchie in her hair, one that looks remarkably like the ones currently on Essie's sales table.

"Yes," I breathe. "You know what she likes?"

"Sure thing." She smiles again, calling the order back to the older woman making coffees, and my relief makes me a little weak at the knees. "She also really likes these." The girl points towards a cabinet beside her that's filled with pastries topped with cream and chocolate and cherries.

"Of course she does," I say, handing over my card with a sigh. "And two of those, please."

When I arrive back at Essie's stall she's wrapping a bunch of items in tissue paper and passing them to her latest customer. Thankfully there's no one else and Essie gets her first breather in over an hour.

I hand her the coffee and she takes it. Her fingers brush

against mine and electricity shoots up my wrist. She inhales the rich coffee scent and sighs.

"You touched me," she says, eyes flicking up to meet mine, her mouth forming a wicked curve.

I nearly choke on my sip of coffee. "You touched *me*, Estella," I drawl. "Leave my innocent hands out of this."

The corner of her mouth tugs up even further, into something one might call a smile, but I know better.

"Here," I say, handing her the box in my hands.

Her eyes flash to mine then to the box, excitement in them.

"Yesssss," she groans, opening the lid. "I always get there too late and miss out. Thank you." She actually means it. There's real sincerity in her voice. "How did you know?"

"The girl at the coffee place may have dropped a hint or two," I say, and feel more than smug when Essie's laugh bounces around me. "Have a sit while you get the chance. Does anything need doing?"

Chapter Fifteen

ESSIE

I SIP at my coffee and watch as Jax (Jax!) moves quietly around the stall, restocking my baskets, laying out more dresses, straightening everything as he goes.

I'm finding it hard to hate him in this moment, drinking coffee and eating pastries he bought for me while helping me at a market.

I usually attend these things solo, with my parents thinking it's not a real job and my friends usually busy on the weekends.

Occasionally Brooke will come with me, but she's easily distracted by all the other things to look at – by which I mean Lisa, the coffee girl who expertly upsold Jax to buying pastries.

But Jax is still here. Helping. He even agreed to man the stall for the ten minutes I rushed to the bathroom. I swore I'd only be five but the line was long. When I got back he was busy chatting away to a young mum with a pigtailed daughter who would not accept that the dresses were too small for her.

"Essie does do custom ones," he was saying as I hurried up. "I'm sure she could do one in her size."

"I'm so sorry. The line," I breathed, before turning to the woman and smiling at her. "How can I help?"

The woman ordered two dresses and bought a handful of headbands and scrunchies for gifts.

Then, in the next lull, Jax insisted I sit down again while he did another tidy-up of the tables. He was being startlingly helpful, and being around him wasn't a hostile standoff like I'd thought it was going to be. In fact, it was … enjoyable?

"Jax?" A new voice. It startles me out of my contemplation of him. Have I been too harsh?

He glances up at his name. "Cayley!" I look to the newcomer, and sure enough, it's Melissa's older sister, who is so cool and gorgeous and intimidating I choke on pastry crumbs.

She hugs him. "What on earth are you doing here?"

He slides his hands into his jeans pockets and ducks his head a little. Is he embarrassed? Regardless, he looks cute standing there somewhat bashful. "Ah, Essie had car trouble so I gave her a ride. They locked us in before I could get out again, so I figured I'd try and make myself useful. She hasn't thrown anything at me yet so I must be doing okay," he says, his voice and smile easy and light. He shoots me a look with his last sentence, an eyebrow lifted, and this time, instead of feeling like he's laughing at me, I feel like he's laughing with me.

"I've come close a couple of times," I say with a smile before I have a chance to wonder what is going on with the way he's looking at me. "But the coffee saved your butt."

Cayley bursts out laughing. "Hey, Essie," she says and for some reason I blush. It's one of those 'I can't believe she knows my name' moments. "Do you make all this stuff?" I nod. "And most of your outfits, right?"

I nod again, lost for words.

"It's pretty impressive, right?" Jax says, saving me from my awkward silence.

"Do you do other dresses?" Cayley asks, her face thoughtful. "Like, for example, bridesmaid dresses?"

"For you?" Jax asks, and Cayley nods.

"The dresses Mum ordered for us aren't going to be ready in time. The lady had a total screw-up."

They both turn to me, still standing there like a big awkward dork. "Umm, maybe?" I say. "It depends what you want and when for. And fabrics, I guess. Some are harder to get than others, especially if you're after a really particular colour. And would it be an existing pattern or would it be something I draft, like a custom design?" I snap my mouth shut, realising I'm blabbering but not really saying anything.

"The wedding is the middle of January. I could find some pictures. Maybe we could meet up and decide if it's doable? You make such gorgeous outfits, I'd love if you could do them and save us from something nasty Mum wants to get online."

I blush again. "Yeah, sounds good."

Jax hands her one of my business cards and Cayley hugs him again, promising me she'll text to set up a meeting time.

"Oh my God," I say as she walks away.

"What?" Jax turns to me, eyes questioning as the realisation hits me.

"I can't do it," I say, turning away and blinking rapidly before the disappointment turns to tears.

"Why not?"

"Because," I say, spinning back to face him, "I can't. I'm not good enough to sew bridesmaid dresses. And not two of them by January!" *Especially if Mum expects me to get a summer job,*

I think, but don't say aloud. My voice is shaky and I'm so relieved there's no one near the stall right now.

"Estella." His voice is that low serious tone again. "We've all seen what you can do. Look at how many people are ordering dresses from you today. Look at the clothes you make for yourself. Meet with Cayley, talk about what she wants and if you really can't do it, make the decision then. But don't brush it aside now without properly considering it. Yeah it's a big deal, but this is what you want to do, isn't it?"

I can see his hand hovering in my peripheral vision, like he wants to touch me in some reassuring way, but he doesn't and I miss it, even though I've never felt his touch in that way before. How can I miss it when I've never experienced it?

My phone bleeps on the table and Jax holds it up. A message from an unknown number is on the screen. "That's Cayley's number," he says, glancing at it briefly then holding it out to me.

I take the phone from him.

> I hope I didn't push you into agreeing, but I'd really love to catch up about the dresses. I love your wardrobe and want a part of it! Does tomorrow work for you? If it helps, budget is really not a concern at this point. Or I'll beg, and buy you coffee?

I read the text three times, then lower the phone and lift my gaze to meet Jax's. "She really wants me to do it."

"Of course she does. Estella, you're good. Accept it."

A smile starts slowly, then I'm grinning at him and he grins back. "Oh my God, I can't believe it. I've always wanted to do bridesmaid dresses." I do a weird little run on the spot to release some of my excitement and he laughs, but again, he's not mocking me. He steps away, turning as he goes.

"Jax," I reach out and my hand lands on his arm. The bare skin beneath my fingertips is warm and smooth. The tingles that shoot up my arm make me a little dizzy. His eyes land on my hand and he blows out a sharp little breath. "Thank you," I manage to breathe before ripping my hand off his skin like I've been scalded.

Chapter Sixteen

JAX

I THINK ESSIE IS A WITCH. Or someone who can conjure flame. Or something. Because my arm still burns from where she touched it.

The day is flying by and even Essie's huge boxes of stock are running low. Mind you, she has been selling up an absolute storm, so I can see why.

It got to the point where I was wrapping up her sales for her and taking payments while she moved on to the next customers. I have no idea how she would have coped without me, which I'd never mention aloud because it makes me sound extremely self-involved.

The girl from the coffee cart dropped by around one o'clock with more coffee and sandwiches.

Essie hugged her after squealing hello and thanked her profusely. She officially introduced us and I smiled and thanked Lisa for the tips earlier in the day.

But now numbers are beginning to thin out. The crowds are going home because their children are cranky or they've spent their allocated budgets.

"Okay if I go for a quick look around?" I ask Essie as she waves off another customer and straightens the table again.

"Yeah, sure," she says. "You know I was planning to be here by myself, you didn't need to stick around."

I can't tell if she's mad at me for it or not. "I didn't mind. It's been … weirdly fun."

"You're weird," she says with a smirk and I roll my eyes, laughing before heading off around the park to see what else is on offer.

I buy a few artisan food things for Cayley's mum's Christmas present and spend far too long poring over a hand-made jewellery stall and one that specialises in fancy metalwork decor.

I buy a box of fudge that I intend to share with Essie when I get back to our stall.

Our stall. As if I have any real part in it. Though it has felt good, working alongside her, chatting aimlessly about random things in the few brief quiet times.

I stop short as she comes into view. She's got this adorable flush on her cheeks and she's gazing upward … at Jeremy.

I swear.

She giggles and I hate it. I stalk closer and Essie's eyes flick towards me. She bites her lip, nods at Jeremy, hands him one of her business cards. He leans down and kisses her cheek, hand coming to rest against her waist for a brief moment, and I want to kneecap him.

I take a deep breath, exhaling slowly as I avert my eyes. It's easier not to look.

"Jax." Jeremy gives me a nod as he walks past, a smug little smile on his face as he twirls the card bearing Essie's phone number between his fingers. I give him a silent nod in return and he strides away. Essie watches him go.

"What does he want?" I mutter as I drop the box of fudge on the table, barely missing one of the more expensive dresses laid out there. I wince as I realise my mistake, but it's gone before Essie turns her eyes on me, glaring.

"Not that it's your business, but he was asking me out," she snaps. "And watch where you're putting that sticky crap near the dresses."

I snatch the box back up. "Sorry," I say, but I know as the word comes out it's wrong.

It's not the wrong word, but I've said it wrong, with too much resentment and sarcasm because my gut is twisting and bitterness is roiling through me at the thought of him being allowed to touch her, and me not.

She glares at me for a moment longer and I can't even meet those brilliant green eyes. I can't bear to see the fury I know is in them. Because Essie never lands somewhere in the middle. Not with me, anyway. That brief exchange, my raging jealousy, and we're back to where we started.

I've managed to wipe out an entire day of making her smile with five words.

The rest of the day limps along. It's definitely not flying anymore. Thankfully the market was nearly done when Jeremy showed his face. I'm somewhat satisfied to know that Essie hasn't received a single text or phone call since he took her card, but even thinking that makes me feel awful. She checks her phone a few times, sliding it silently back onto the table when she realises there no new alerts and her disappointment hurts almost as much as upsetting her earlier.

By four o'clock we're done, and I silently help Essie pack up her remaining stock. There's hardly anything left. She's made an absolute killing today. If the interaction earlier hadn't set us back on such an awful footing I'd probably have the nerve to ask if she would consider it a good day, ask her if she was happy with how it went.

But considering she's barely acknowledging me again, I keep my mouth shut.

Lisa from the coffee cart calls past before they leave, bringing a couple of pieces of brownie with her. "Tell Brooke hi from me," she says to Essie.

"I can give you her phone number and you can say hi yourself," Essie replies, those lips curved into a knowing smile.

Lisa blushes and stammers but takes the proffered scrap of paper Essie scribbles a phone number on. "Thanks," she whispers. "We'll have to catch up soon," she says, voice still low. Her eyes flicker in my direction and I pretend I didn't notice and am not totally eavesdropping on their conversation.

I hear Essie snort. "Trust me, there's nothing to catch up on."

Lisa laughs. "Sure. We still need a proper catch up regardless."

"Yes, we do," Essie says. "I'll text you."

They hug each other and Lisa heads back to the coffee cart, which I can see now the crowds have dispersed and a couple of stalls have already begun packing up. A woman, who I'm assuming is Lisa's mother, is closing up the cart, latching the serving window shut.

Essie watches Lisa walk away then turns to the gazebo,

starting to collapse it. She doesn't ask for my help. But I'm not a complete jackass, so I help her regardless.

Chapter Seventeen

ESSIE

I'VE CHANGED my outfit five times.

I'm not even leaving the house. But Cayley is coming over soon to discuss the bridesmaid dresses with me. She's bringing her mum, the bride, with her.

She texted me a bunch of pictures last night, along with a link to her wedding Pinterest board. I was up half the night with ideas racing through my head, trying to get some of them recorded on paper. I spent all morning trying to refine those late-night designs.

I've finally settled on an outfit. For now, anyway. It's a lilac sundress with a gathered skirt and ruffled straps. It's pretty and also a bit classy.

Every fibre of my being screamed at me to go at it with makeup. It's my armour, but I'm meeting with a bride. I don't want to look too edgy, so I manage to restrain myself and settle for the barest pearly pink eyeshadow and not a touch of eyeliner.

I carry a basket of fabric samples and my sketches downstairs, along with my laptop so I can look up more images if we need to.

Jax and David are sitting at the table when I walk into the kitchen. I don't even know why David is home; he's usually gone most of the afternoon, right through to evening.

I heard Jax come home not long ago. He's showered away the grime of the engineering workshop, his hair damp, and he's wearing a faded blue t-shirt and jeans, bare forearms resting on the table beside his stack of textbooks. I really thought he'd have more of a life than this, but all he ever seems to do is work, study and drive me places.

My eyes linger on his arms and I remember the feel of firm muscle under my fingertips yesterday, when I thanked him for talking me into accepting the job.

Right before he ruined everything by being a jerk over Jeremy again. I don't understand Jax's problem with him.

David barely looks up, but Jax's gaze lands on me and stays. I watch as he notices the basket clutched against my belly, my hair braided into a ponytail falling over one shoulder and finally my dress.

He opens his mouth as if he's going to say something, but I turn away, dumping my basket on the kitchen bench.

"I need the kitchen, please," I announce.

"Well, we're here," David says, not even looking at me. I scowl at the back of his head.

Jax flips his workbook closed. "Come on man, we can go somewhere else."

"Or Essie can go somewhere else," David mutters.

My face heats and my eyes burn. I do not want to do this right now. I don't have time to fight with David and get myself under control.

"Someone's coming over and I need the table," I say, willing my voice to stay calm, to not wobble.

Jax's head flicks in my direction, then away again.

"I don't care, Ess," David says, his voice bored. "I have to make dinner soon. You and your friends can go play somewhere else."

My hands are shaking. I clench them around the handles of the basket and take a deep breath.

"Estella," Jax drawls and David sniggers. I ignore my brother and turn to Jax. "Cayley?" He mouths the question and I give a quick nod. He tilts his head, towards the hallway to the office. "Use my room," he says.

David scoffs. "Don't go out of your way for her."

I don't want to use Jax's room. I don't want to accept this stupid gesture of kindness. But I don't have time left to fight with David over the kitchen.

I flex my fingers on the basket. I glance at David, who has barely looked up during this whole exchange. I flick my gaze back to Jax and our eyes lock. He hasn't looked away, not the entire time I've been in the room.

I nod and he rolls out of his seat, standing in one smooth movement. He stretches an arm over his head and the hem of his t-shirt parts ways with his jeans.

My face flares hot again, but for entirely different reasons. There's no anger or frustration in this blush.

Jax heads for his room, gesturing me to follow him. I'm apprehensive about what state the room will be in. Cayley and her mum will be here any minute so I don't have time to clean it up.

Jax pushes open the door with a flourish and I step around him, catching a whiff of his freshly showered scent that makes my stomach bottom out. I stare around, gobsmacked. The room is immaculate. He must have stacked all his boxes inside the cupboards I emptied of my fabric.

"Woah," I say, and Jax chuckles. "You're very tidy."

He laughs louder and steps over to the neatly made bed, folding it away into a couch with a few movements.

I like watching his hands move.

I drag over the little coffee table that Jax has been using as a bedside table. He sweeps up the book, phone charger and other little bits and pieces – some coins, a pencil – and slips them into the cupboard in the corner.

"When I can't find them later, remind me that I put them there," he says, giving me a little smile. "Estella," his voice softens. "About yester—"

A knock at the door and my corresponding yelp cuts him off. Blood is pounding through my veins, making me dizzy. I'm not sure if it's the way Jax is standing there, hands hanging by his sides, saying my name like that, or if it's to do with who's on the other side of the door and what it might mean for my little business.

Jax shakes his head. "Never mind. Go."

I glance around the room, making sure everything is ready, then take a deep breath and rush to answer the door.

Cayley is standing there in a yellow t-shirt and white shorts and I almost swoon with how fabulous she looks. The woman beside her is obviously her mother. She gives me a warm smile, says hello and introduces herself as Kate.

Cayley steps forward and wraps me in a one-armed hug. Her other arm is wrapped around a thick binder I can only assume contains wedding plans. She smells like sunshine and flowers.

"I'm so excited," she says, stepping back.

I gesture for them to come inside and lead them down the hall. As we pass the kitchen Jax calls out.

"Hey, Aunt Kate," he says, poking his head around the door with a grin.

"Hello, Jax," she says.

"Don't leave without saying goodbye," he says, that charming smile not faltering for a second.

"Of course not," she says.

"And you'll have to show me what magic Essie is working on. I know it'll be perfect."

He turns his smile on me and it softens slightly, but the charm is still there.

I smile back without realising I'm even doing it until his mouth hitches higher.

When the hell did I start thinking Jax's smile is charming?

Chapter Eighteen

JAX

ESSIE, Aunt Kate and Cayley have been shut in my room for well over an hour.

I try to study but my mind keeps wandering down the hallway, wondering how it's going. Something must be going right or my aunt and cousin would be long gone.

Or maybe they're still going through the massive folder Cayley was hugging to her chest with every tiny detail about the wedding in it.

I give up on study when David finally starts making dinner. He's banging around making it impossible to concentrate, rather than just simply difficult.

As soon as I start helping he lets me take over, and before long has somehow vanished, leaving me in charge all over again.

The door opens down the hall and the three women appear. All are smiling, though Essie's is bestowed with some kind of magic. She's glowing, eyes sparkling. The smile doesn't fade even when her eyes meet mine.

I raise an eyebrow in question, and she gives the tiniest nod. I flash her a grin before turning to hug Aunt Kate.

"How'd it go?" I ask her.

She smiles that smile that is so like my mum's. It makes me wish she was here, not hotfooting it through Europe drinking red wine and eating the world's best bread and cheese.

"Wonderful," Kate says, giving Essie a warm smile. "I can't wait to see what Essie's going to do for us. I can't stay, but Jax, come round for dinner or something, okay? Anytime."

"Thanks, Kate," I say, suddenly ridiculously wistful for my family. It's been only Mum and me for so long, but Kate, Cayley and Melissa have always been part of our lives, with Mum and Kate leaning on each other to get through the rough parts of single parenting. We even lived together for a little while, right after Cayley's dad passed away.

Essie walks my family to the door and she's still beaming when she returns to the kitchen.

"It went well, then?" I ask, almost too afraid to look at her.

"It did," she says, her voice a little breathless, like she can't quite believe it happened. She pauses while she pulls herself up to sit on the edge of the bench, and before I have a chance to think of something to say to fill the silence she speaks again, her tone turned serious. "You don't think they're only going along with it because they're nice people and don't want me to feel bad? Or because they're your family and don't want you to be homeless?"

I laugh and she scowls at me. "I wouldn't be homeless. I'd go live with them, even though there's nowhere near enough space for that."

Her scowl deepens. "So they only want to go ahead so you

won't end up on their couch?" Her mouth twitches, like she's fighting back a smile, but her eyes are tinged with worry.

"Estella, no," I say, leaning my hip against the counter beside her. She turns to look at me and I have to tilt my chin up to look her in the eye. I enjoy it far more than I should. "They want you to make the dresses because you're good. I saw those sketches. They're perfect for the kind of wedding they're having."

She zones out, chewing her bottom lip and like every time I see her doing it, I want to reach out and free it.

I'm not going to put my hands on you, Estella, not unless I'm one hundred percent sure that you want me too.

My words echo back at me. Then David's.

Don't hit on her, man. It's too weird … Have fun tonight, but not with my sister.

I've backed myself into a corner and there's no way out. Even if by some miracle Essie one day lets me touch her, I've promised David that I won't go there. I'm not even supposed to flirt with her. Not that I consciously flirt with anyone. It seems to happen of its own accord, especially when Essie's around.

But at least for the moment, Essie isn't shouting at me or trying to murder me with her eyes. She's simply sitting here beside me, sharing her insecurities with me.

It makes me feel … special.

Essie casts a certain persona into the world: this bold, fiery girl who cares little what anyone thinks of her. But the more time I spend with her, the more I'm learning of her apprehension about so many things. The realisation that she's letting me, of all people, see her insecurities is like being wrapped in a warm blanket.

Usually I only get the fun, flirty side of girls, and then their tears when it's over.

With Essie, I'm getting the opposite. I wonder if she even realises the ways she's letting me in.

"I hope so," she says eventually, focusing her gaze on the kitchen again, bringing her eyes to rest on mine.

"I know so," I say, leaning in close. I let my hand rest on the bench, right beside her hip, as if to prove to her that I want to touch her but won't until she asks. Or to prove to myself that I can exist this close to her without crossing that final line.

The sound of the door has Essie pushing herself off the bench, breaking the eye contact. I blink a few times, readjusting my eyes to force them to focus on something else.

"I'll go get my stuff out of your room," she says softly. "And Jax?" I turn to face her where she's paused, halfway out of the room. "Thank you."

I'm still smiling at the empty doorway when her dad, Karl, walks into the room.

"Hey, Jax," he says in that solid deep voice of his. "I thought David was on dinner tonight?"

I shrug. "We're both doing it," I say, just as David reappears from the opposite direction Essie went in.

"Hey, Dad," he says. "Dinner's almost ready."

I give him some shifty side-eye before turning away, finishing the salad I was working on before Essie finished her meeting.

Essie bustles back through the kitchen a few minutes later, carrying her basket back to her room, and her mum arrives a few minutes after that. The table is set – at least David is useful in some regard – and we sit down to eat.

"David, honey, could you call your sister, please?" Miriam, his mum, asks.

David grunts but gets up from the table. He steps into the hallway and shouts up the stairs. "Ess, hurry up! Dinner time." Miriam winces and shares a look with Karl that says, 'I could have done that.'

"I'm coming!" she shouts back.

David slumps back into his seat and Essie thunders down the stairs a few moments later, tumbling into her seat across from me.

She glances up and catches me watching her and for the first time in the week we've been sitting across from each other for dinner, she smiles back. It's only there for a second, but it's still a smile.

Conversation begins to flow, the usual family dinnertime conversation about what everyone did that day and what's coming up later in the week.

"How's the job hunt going, Ess?" Miriam asks, and Essie freezes across the table from me.

"I've got an interview in the morning," she mutters, and her mother beams at her.

"Really? That's fantastic."

"Wait. What?" My filter has vanished on me again and I realise I've spoken the words aloud. Essie's gaze flicks to mine and she gives me the tiniest shake of her head.

But I ignore it.

There's a hot feeling in my gut, and it's far different from the usual hot feeling I get when I think about Essie. "When are you going to do the dresses if you've got a job?"

"I'll find time," she says, her voice tight.

Karl chuckles as if trying to diffuse the sudden tension at

the table. "Essie can't spend her whole summer in her room making a few dresses," he says, and I bristle at his dismissiveness.

"It's not just a few dresses, though," I say.

"Jax, don't," Essie mutters at me across the table. Her shoulders are slumped, head down as she toys with the lettuce on her plate.

"Look, Jax, we know Essie has done fairly well at some markets recently, but there's a big gap in the calendar for those until well after Christmas," Miriam says to me. "It's an expectation in this family to get a summer job. Not only does it earn her money to spend on her fabrics and things, but it's excellent to put on her C.V. for the future."

David butts into the conversation. "It's not a big deal," he says. "Essie's just being dramatic about it, as usual."

Essie flinches at that, but keeps her eyes locked on her plate. Not a spark of her usual fire.

I stare at Miriam, Karl and David for a moment, taking them in as they carry on completely oblivious to the effect their words are having, aware my mouth is hanging open a little and I must look like a real fool.

"I understand that," I say. "But I'm not sure any of you understand quite what Essie is doing." There's silence around the table, and when I dare a glance at David he's watching me with suspicion written all over his face. "Essie's not spending her days making a couple of baby dresses and hair things to sell at markets. Yes, that's part of it. But that's only the beginning. Do you know that yesterday she sold over fifty of those dresses? And took at least ten orders for custom dresses? That's not to mention the commission she got this afternoon for two bridesmaid dresses. It's not a hobby. Essie's running an actual business and that's going to look better on a C.V. than a part-time summer job."

I end my tirade and shovel a forkful of food into my mouth to stop me continuing.

There's utter silence except for my chewing and the scrape of my fork against my plate as I ready the next mouthful of food.

"Well," Miriam says eventually, clearing her throat. "If that's true, it appears we don't fully understand what Essie's been up to." She turns her gaze on Essie. "Maybe we'll talk about it later, okay?"

Essie nods silently while I try not to bristle at Miriam's "if that's true" comment, and the meal resumes. Once everyone has returned to normal conversation Essie finally lifts her gaze to mine. Her face is void of expression and I lift the corner of my mouth in a tight smile, hoping to provoke some kind of reaction from her, preferably a positive one.

I watch as she exhales slowly and my heart leaps as her lips curve upwards.

It's only after she looks away that I realise what the slight shimmer along her lashes is.

Chapter Nineteen

ESSIE

I HAVE UNDERESTIMATED JACKSON SHERWOOD.

The realisation struck me at dinner time, when he stood up to my entire family on my behalf and told them the realities of my business.

I'd never really enlightened my parents on my success. It's something I've held pretty close to my chest the whole way along. Even Brooke doesn't understand the full extent of it.

That it's a real business.

That I'm really good at it.

That customers come back to me time and time again as their children or grandchildren grow out of one size of dress and they want bigger ones.

Not a single person in my life has ever mentioned that I design the dresses myself. Nobody mentions that the majority of the clothes I sew for myself are from self-drafted patterns. Yes, I make the clothes, but I also design them.

I took textiles at school; in Year 10, when we could choose a couple of option interest classes to see if we wanted to pursue them. I was the only one in my class who could already sew, because my nana taught me when I was six. When she died I inherited her sewing machine. It was old, but it was functional. It's the machine I still use now.

I ended up dropping the textiles class in favour of classes that would help me run a business.

It had the added benefit of pleasing my parents – because business- or science-based subjects always gain their approval – which doesn't happen often, so I have to take the wins where I can.

My mind is scattered as I clear the table. David vanished the second the meal was over, even though I know his contribution to cooking was the barest minimum. Somehow Jax ended up doing it. Not that I'm complaining. Jax is a way better cook than my brother.

My parents have wandered into the lounge, where they'll watch TV or play cards for the rest of the evening. I consider joining them once I've finished cleaning up, but I'm not sure I'm ready to talk about my business.

I also don't want them to ask too many questions about the job interview I have lined up for tomorrow.

The interview is at my favourite fabric store, which is definitely a detail I'm planning to conveniently leave out of the conversation for as long as possible. It's not a job that would be a hardship to me. I'd get to talk about sewing and fabric and patterns all day. And it's only part-time, so I should still have plenty of time to do the sewing I need to on all my commissions. Who needs sleep?

But I know my parents will still frown upon it. Because anything I actually want to do is never good enough for them.

Jax and I move around each other in the kitchen as I stack

the dishwasher and he wipes down the benches. We work in silence, but it's not bitter and uncomfortable. It's pleasant and … friendly.

We finish our tasks at the same time and end up facing each other in the middle of the kitchen, a metre or so between us.

Before I can think of what to say, how to thank him, my phone chimes with a text message and my hand automatically reaches for it.

It's an unknown number, which isn't that unusual considering how many people I give business cards to.

> Hi Ess. Jeremy here. Was good to see you yesterday. Any chance you're free tonight?

My breath hitches and I smile at the screen.

He texted.

Finally.

I was starting to give up hope; that he'd only asked for my number at the market yesterday to be polite because it seemed the appropriate thing to do after making out with someone at a party.

Little zinging sensations fire through my body as I think about Friday night, and about the way Jeremy's eyes lingered on me yesterday.

Sure am, I reply. What do you have in mind?

His reply comes immediately. I was thinking beach?

Glancing up from my phone, I realise Jax is gone. Damn, I need to say something to him, need to thank him.

Instead, I poke my head into the lounge.

"Okay if I use the car for a bit?" I ask my parents. "I'm

going out to the beach to meet a friend." I give them the details I know they'll ask for.

"Oh, okay, sure," Mum says. 'Don't be too late, though."

I nod. "I won't be."

"All right honey, be safe."

I bolt up the stairs before anyone has a chance to change their minds or ask more questions about where I'm going and who I'm meeting.

I text Jeremy back, telling him I'll meet him there. I don't want the fallout from my parents, David *and* Jax that would no doubt occur if Jeremy were to turn up at my house.

In my room, I rummage through my drawers, excited to wear the new bikini I made a few weeks ago. It's emerald green and purple and I've been waiting for a chance to wear it. I pull it on, tying the halter strap behind my neck, then reach for the dress I was wearing. The green strap peeking out from under the lilac will be cute.

But my hand veers away and instead I grab denim shorts and throw on a black t-shirt with a low V-neck. Maybe for once I don't want to be admired for 'not caring what other people think of me' and the way I dress. Today I want to blend in. It feels easier.

Grabbing a beach towel and a cardigan – it's still warm outside now, but the evenings get cold, especially at the beach – I head towards the garage, which takes me down the hall past Jax's room.

I pause outside, unsure if I should interrupt him. The door's slightly ajar though so I step closer, nudging it a fraction wider.

He's sitting at the desk I usually sew at, the books for his course open and spread across the surface.

His elbow is propped on the desk, chin resting in his hand, headphones covering his ears. The evening sun filters in through the tree outside the window and he's lit up golden. All the words I'd thought of to say to him vanish at the sight.

I stand there for a moment longer, knowing I'm being weird, before turning away and heading for the car.

I push the image of Jax sitting there in the sunlight to the recesses of my mind and bury it in several thousand worries about seeing Jeremy, whether he'll think I'm fun and funny, or simply odd, and if I can actually sew two beautiful dresses in less than two months.

Chapter Twenty

JAX

"DUDE."

I startle as David steps into my line of vision and pull my headphones off.

"Oh, hey," I say, trying to pretend he didn't give me a huge fright.

"What's going on with you and my sister?"

"What?" My eyes flick to the desk in front of me, the scattered bits of paper and all my workbooks. I breathe a bit easier when I realise the scrap of paper I've been sketching the side of a girl's face on is hidden from sight. Because the girl's face I was sketching was Essie's.

I turn to face David as he sprawls on the couch, which I haven't yet returned to its bed state. "There's nothing going on with me and Essie."

He gives me an eye roll, and despite feeling the heat building at the back of my neck I continue to play it cool.

"Dinner time," he says.

I shrug. I can't explain it without sounding like there's something going on.

"And she was just standing outside your room."

My eyes flick to the door, as though she's still standing there. My heart skips in my chest. "What? Like right now?"

David nods. "Yeah, when I came down the hall. She was standing right there watching you, then she took off somewhere."

"Oh." I don't really have anything to say to that, either. Why was she there? Had she wanted to talk about what happened at dinner?

"Is she bothering you? You can tell her to stop. Or I will if you don't want to be mean to her."

"She's fine," I say, my voice tight. I don't need David interfering on my behalf, especially when I don't want Essie to back off at all. If anything, I want to see more of her.

"How did you know about her business?" He says the word business with such heavy sarcasm I want to throw something at him.

Has he always been this much of a smug jerk, or has he got worse as he's got older? Maybe it's university. Both he and Jeremy seem to be bigger jerks than ever after their year away. I don't remember David being like this before, but then he only ever seems to behave like this when it's to do with Essie. And his parents' behaviour towards her isn't much better at times. It's obvious they love her and want her to succeed, but I get the feeling her definition of success is different to theirs.

I think back to when we were younger, when David and I would be playing soccer in the backyard and Essie would come tearing through the middle of our game, cartwheeling and singing, shrieking and giggling, always dressed in a sparkly dress or outrageous colour combination.

There has always been this opinion that Essie is *a lot*, that she's *too much*, overly dramatic. The comments were always indulgent. Like yes, she's loud and likes things done her way, but one day she'll grow up and settle down.

Except she hasn't. She's grown up, for sure, but as far as I can tell she's got bolder and even more fiery and she's definitely not scared to share her opinion.

The more time I'm spending with her though, the more I'm learning that a lot of that is a front, and it makes me mad.

Mad that the things that make her special and unique are what's used against her, that she feels she has to make herself smaller and less vibrant to fit in, that she even worries about these kinds of things instead of going out there being bright and bold and brave all the time.

I realise I've been drifting and David is still waiting for me answer. I sigh. I don't want to do this with him. "I drove her to that market yesterday because her car wouldn't start and she had no way to get there."

"And?"

God, he's being such a dick. "And we got there really late. My car got locked in. I wasn't allowed to leave, so I stayed and helped her."

"Aw, sorry man." David grimaces. "What a way to have to spend your weekend."

I sigh. "You know, spending time with your sister isn't actually a hardship."

He laughs, a harsh, bitter sound. It's obvious he doesn't think what I said is funny, but he doesn't believe me either. "Yeah, right."

"It's not," I insist, though I don't know why. "She's funny and smart and heaps of fun."

"I thought you said there was nothing going on."

I grit my teeth. This conversation is going to go nowhere. Such a good validation of my character when my best mate can't believe I can enjoy spending time with a girl without being into her. The fact I'm actually very into Essie is irrelevant right now. "There isn't anything going on," I say through my teeth. "In case you haven't noticed, she barely tolerates my presence."

"So you're into her, but she's playing hard to get? Man, I told you not to hit on her." He pulls a face, like he wants to vomit.

"What the hell, dude?" I toss my hands in the air and spin away from him. I have a fleeting second of awesomeness that the chair I'm on is a spinning office chair and the moment is appropriately dramatic and exasperated. I turn back once I've had a moment to collect myself.

"There is nothing going on, from either side. I wouldn't even call us friends. I'm not hitting on her and she's not playing hard to get. I was helping her out. That's it!" I don't notice my voice is rising as I speak, but I end on a shout.

David pushes himself off the couch. "Whatever you say, Jax. Maybe it's time you found someone to hit on. A rebound might be good for you. I know Annie screwed you over, but you've been spending too much time with my sister. You're getting all dramatic like her."

My pen hits the door frame seconds after he's left the room.

Chapter Twenty-One

ESSIE

I PULL into a free space in the beach carpark, considering the other vehicles lined up and wondering which of them belongs to Jeremy.

It's a gorgeous evening, the sun barely beginning its descent.

Sliding my sandals off, I breathe a deep sigh as my toes touch the sun-warmed sand. A gentle, salty breeze caresses my face, whipping a few strands of hair free of my braid.

For a moment I forget why I'm there. I forget all about Jeremy and settle into the feelings the beach gives me, helping me centre myself and release the tension from things at home and the anxiety over the meeting with Kate and Cayley.

Inhaling deeply, enjoying the salty tang, I survey the beach sprawled out in both directions. There's a large group of people not far down, maybe twenty or so sitting around in beach chairs, a couple sprawled on towels. My gaze skitters over them before I turn to check the other direction for Jeremy. An older couple walking a dog, a toddler and woman I can only assume is her mother, a girl barely older than me running.

I can't see him anywhere.

I check my phone and on the screen is a message telling me he's already arrived. I'm typing out a reply, asking where he is, when a figure detaches from the large group, heading towards me.

My heart seizes when I make out Jeremy's gelled blonde hair and wide grin.

I have seriously misjudged this situation.

"Hey, you," Jeremy says as he reaches me, wrapping me into a hug and lifting me off the ground.

"Hey," I say, plastering on a smile and hoping my voice doesn't wobble too much.

"Come meet everyone," he says, taking my hand after he's gently placed my feet back on the sand.

"Who's everyone?" I ask, slipping down the soft dune in his wake.

"It's a bunch of people I work with and their partners and stuff." Jeremy's still holding my hand, helping me stay upright. He doesn't appear to have noticed my unease.

I'm okay with people, when I have a clear purpose of what I'm supposed to talk to them about, and when I'm prepared. I can chat to people all day long at a market, because I know my product inside out and know the best way to help my customers.

Making small talk with strangers … I'm never at my best.

Jeremy waves a hand to indicate everyone, turning to me. "This is everyone. Hey, everyone," he calls, gaining the attention of the group, "this is Essie."

A few waves, a few hellos, smiles all round before they turn back to their own conversations. I'm relieved, because I felt my face heat the second Jeremy made me centre of attention.

"Want to sit?" Jeremy indicates a plaid picnic blanket spread over the sand. "Do you want anything to drink?"

"Uh, sure, what have you got?" I tuck my knees under me as I settle onto the blanket.

He pulls a beer out of a nearby chilly bin.

"Um, I can't have that and drive home," I say.

"Oh, right," Jeremy says, rummaging about in the chilly bin again. "Coke or Sprite?"

I reach out for the Sprite, thanking him as he sprawls beside me, the beer still in his hand. He twists off the cap, tossing it at a guy sitting on a camp chair next to us. The guy rolls his eyes and mock-glares at Jeremy, his eyes lingering on me as his gaze glides past.

I readjust my position while Jeremy takes a long pull of beer. "So, um, where do you work? What do you actually do?"

He grins up at me, resting his head on a propped elbow. "I work at TechCo, in sales."

I nod. TechCo is a huge technology department store. "Do you work in a particular department?"

"Yeah, TV and audio for me." He points across the group, marking a few others. "They're in my department." He points to a few more. "Kitchen." And a few more. "Whiteware and large appliances."

"And who are all the others?" I ask, since he's barely covered half the group.

"Partners, friends, associated acquaintances." He shrugs like it doesn't really matter. Which I suppose it doesn't. It's not like I'm going to see these people again. Jeremy runs a hand up my arm, trailing his fingers along my skin. "How've you been? Was the market good?"

I nod and smile. "Yeah, the market was great. It was busy

and I sold so much." I trail off as I notice Jeremy grinning and waving to a new arrival. He wasn't even listening.

"Oh, sorry, babes," he says, turning back to me. "That's so great. I'm glad you had a good day."

He tips his beer bottle back and in another gulp finishes the bottle. I don't think I've ever seen someone drink a beer that fast.

"Wanna walk with me?" He trails his fingers higher this time, catching some of my flyaway hair and tucking it behind my ear. I shiver slightly at the touch and nod, allowing the movement to tip my head into his palm.

Jeremy climbs to his feet and holds out a hand. Taking it, I'm pulled to my feet and he leads me away from the group, with a couple of loud whoops following us. Jeremy gestures rudely back in their direction before tucking me into his side, his hand settling on my waist.

As we walk, we talk. He asks about my holidays, my favourite food and my business. I ask about his job, his family, his plans for next year.

At that question he loses his easy smile, stopping and tugging me to a halt beside him. "Look, Essie, I do really like you, but I'm out of here again at the end of the summer, so this can't be anything serious."

I shrug. "Who says I want anything serious?" I say, feigning casual. Because I've never been in this situation. I don't know what he means.

What is 'this'? The only boyfriends I've ever had asked me out before we ever touched. Then we never actually went anywhere together, only ever as a group. We only went as far as some really bad kissing, so this thing with Jeremy is entirely new to me. We've already done more – and better kissing –

than any relationship I've had before. What does he actually want from me?

He laughs softly and steps closer. "Good, because I like hanging out with you. You're gorgeous and funny. Winning combo." He leans down and kisses me before I have the chance to blush. His mouth is warm and his tongue tastes like beer as it brushes past mine. I get swept away in the rush of butterflies in my stomach but he steps away before I have the chance to get any closer to him.

I glance up and Jeremy is watching me. He unsticks a strand of hair from my cheek and brushes it behind my ear. "God, you're gorgeous," he murmurs softly, then turns to continue walking, twisting his fingers with mine as he does.

We wander for a few minutes in silence before I completely ruin the relaxed, peaceful mood.

"Are you going to tell anyone about this?" I ask, not sure where the question is coming from. Do I want to know the answer? Should I assume and tell people myself, rather than give him the opportunity to say no?

"I don't know," he says. "I haven't really thought about it. Are you going to tell anyone?"

"Well," I say, "David and Jax will likely be dicks about it, but I don't really want it to be a secret."

"Okay, so we'll try and avoid Jax and David finding out, but otherwise we'll see how things go?"

I smile up at him, the ball of anxiety in my stomach releasing again. "Sounds good."

We wander some more, eventually looping around and heading back to where we started, chatting easily and watching the sun dip to the horizon, Jeremy's thumb brushing gently along my skin as we walk. My heart skips beats and my stomach flutters with every soft graze.

I glance at my phone, checking the time, and sigh. "I need to get going," I say, and Jeremy adjusts his course to head for the carpark instead of the group of his workmates and friends.

Pulling my keys from my pocket, I stop beside my car, unsure how to end this. I can't stop fidgeting. I bite down on my lip until it hurts.

Jeremy leans against my car, long legs stretched out in front of him. He guides me to stand between them, his hands on my waist.

Then he pulls me close and kisses me. My heart pounds and my breath comes short. Dizziness washes over me as he pulls my body tight against his, sliding his tongue along my lips. "Sure you can't stay for a little longer?" he whispers, breaking the kiss but sweeping his lips against my cheek, his breath hot against my ear.

Regret fills me. I don't want to leave. I want to stay here and be kissed by this gorgeous guy. I don't want to go home to the negative chaos of my family with their expectations and disappointed looks. "I don't want to go," I whisper back, barely managing to get the words out, "but I have to. I'm sorry."

Jeremy makes a disappointed sound and when I try to step away, he holds me close. "One more," he says, his voice low. He presses into me, tongue tangling with mine, his fingers wound through the base of my braid. I lean into him, almost liquefied in his arms.

It's not one more kiss, it's many, and when he finally releases me, I slide into my car with weak knees, feeling the ghost of the searing heat of his body against mine the entire drive home.

Chapter Twenty-Two

JAX

ESSIE'S WORKING at the kitchen table when I get home from work.

I smile as I pass the kitchen, pausing to watch her feed fabric through her sewing machine.

She glances up and lifts the corner of her mouth into a half-smile when she notices me. "Hey," she says.

"Hi," I say, a little surprised by her friendly greeting, even though we've settled into some sort of truce over the past few days, since the night I defended her to her family. We haven't spoken about it, but Essie is gentler around me, not so quick to bite, and she's generally around more. She'll sit at the counter while I cook, sketching or hand-stitching on a project. Yesterday she had her laptop and swore repeatedly about maths and budgets. I laughed and asked if she needed help, told her I liked maths. It was the first time in a while she'd looked at me in disgust, but it made me laugh even harder.

"Going to shower, be back in a sec," I say now.

"Sure." She turns back to her sewing machine and the stacks of fabric laid out on the table beside her.

I smile to myself and hurry through my shower. Rinsing off the workshop grime is one of the best parts of my day. My job is great but the machine shop is a hot, sweaty, filthy place.

I throw on jeans and a t-shirt and head back to the kitchen. I'm enjoying cooking every day. It's nice to feel a part of the family, like I'm doing something positive to contribute, not only taking up space. I don't really need to start on dinner yet, but it gives me an excuse to hang out with Essie more, which I've been wanting to do as often as possible these days.

The desire to touch her hits me regularly and I find myself having to clench my fists to resist the urge to reach up and experience what the skin of her cheek feels like. I want nothing more in this life than to see what it's like to press my hand against the curve of her waist, in that soft spot above her hipbone and below her ribs. I'm probably deluding myself, but I truly believe it'll be the perfect fit for my palm.

But the situation with Essie is so delicately hanging in the balance there is no way I'm going to push it. Not until I'm one hundred percent sure, anyway. Not after that stupid promise. Though I guess in a way it's been good; it's stopped me pushing it, stopped me from throwing myself at her in desperate need to be wanted.

Essie is feeding more fabric through her machine when I return. She's got a troubled look on her face as she watches the fabric slide through her fingers. There's a clunking noise, and she swears.

"You all right?" I ask.

The fabric appears to be stuck in the machine.

"Yeah," she sighs. "It's jammed. Something doesn't sound quite right, which probably means it needs a service, which I really don't have time for."

"Oh, that sucks," I say, grabbing juice from the fridge. I lift it in her direction but she shakes her head.

"Tea though, please?"

"Your awful pink stuff?"

"Have you tried it, Jackson?" she asks sweetly. "You shouldn't judge until you've tried it."

I laugh. "I know, Estella. There's always more than meets the eye. The smell is enough to put me off, though."

She laughs too and in a few swift, competent movements starts to disassemble the sewing machine.

I watch her hands deftly clean out the machine using a little brush, slipping components in and out of place. Her dark purple sparkly nail polish flashes as she does it and I think of her hands in more ways I shouldn't. I'm going to need to find somewhere else to live or this girl is going to be the death of me. She's so efficient and capable with the machine, and being competent immediately skyrockets on my list of things I'm looking for in a girl. That was something that Annie really wasn't. She needed help with everything.

I set the tea down beside Essie and slide into the seat next to her. "I put some cold water in it," I say as she reaches for the cup, then pauses. At my words she smiles and picks up the cup, bringing it to her lips to blow on it.

Oh man, yep, definitely need to move out.

"This is a lot of fabric," I say, trying to distract myself from the colour of her lipstick.

"You know that job I interviewed for the other day?" she asks, and I nod. "They don't want me to work in the store. They want to sell my stuff." She grins at me, eyes sparkling over the rim of her cup.

"That's awesome! Did you know that going for the interview? Like, was it always about that?"

She shakes her head. "Nope. I went in for an interview for a retail position. But once we got chatting I told them about Starlight Stitches and they'd heard about me. She asked why I wanted a retail job when I could be working on my business, then offered to be a permanent stockist of my items."

I grin. "That's the coolest news. Well done."

"Thanks. And Jax, thanks for the other day. You know, with my parents." She dips her chin as she says it, as though she's embarrassed. I shove my hand under my leg to stop myself lifting her chin right back up again.

"No worries, Estella. Anytime."

Essie fixes her machine, returning to sewing, and I head into the kitchen to start dinner. We work mostly in silence, the only sound coming from Essie's little speaker on the table and one of us occasionally muttering curse words when something goes wrong. A couple of times I catch Essie singing softly and another time she catches me humming tunelessly and moving to the music as though I might be dancing. Which I'm not, but her smirk tells me she believes otherwise. I glare at her and turn away but not before I catch the laughter on her face.

These minutes are perfection.

I'm laying out everything needed to set the table on the bench when Essie's mum gets home. Essie's creations are still spread across the table in tidy piles of fabric in different stages of construction and she's busy working away when Miriam enters the room. She glances at me first, stacking plates on the bench, ready to be transferred to the table when Essie is done, then at her daughter, who hasn't yet looked up. I know from the muttering that Essie's in the middle of a complicated part of the process.

Miriam sighs and drops her work bag onto a chair at the other end of the table to Essie. She'd normally place it on the table, except there isn't room.

"Essie," Miriam says, her voice stern, and already I don't like where this is going. "We've talked about you sewing in here."

Essie finally looks up after finishing her seam. "I know, but there isn't enough space in my room for this."

"Well, Jax has been working all day and has cooked us dinner and he can't even get to the table because you've taken over," Miriam says, and I flinch. I don't want to be used against Essie. "In fact, we've all been working all day. Jax, me, your father, David. We don't really want to have to deal with your hobby when we get home."

"Fine," Essie cries, wrenching the piece of fabric she's finished stitching from the machine. She picks up a basket from under the table and starts flinging her piles into it.

"I assume since we haven't heard anything else about it, the job interview was unsuccessful," Miriam says, and I see Essie glowering at the table as she continues to pack up her things.

"Miriam," I say, hoping to diffuse the tension before Essie completely blows. I've seen her temper; I've seen her react to her parents before. And I don't blame her right now for whatever pain her mum's words are causing. And I won't blame her for blowing up with hurt and rage when she can't endure them anymore.

But maybe I can help. Miriam turns to me and I swallow, words catching in my throat. "What Essie does, it's not really a hobby," I manage to get out.

"Jax, honey, I know you're trying to be kind to Essie, but she needs to accept the expectations and stop throwing tantrums when she's asked to. Also, this is a family matter. Perhaps it's better if you give us a moment alone."

"I am not throwing a tantrum," Essie says, forcing her voice to remain low, "and Jax, you don't have to go. It's fine. I'm packing up then I'll come and set the table for you."

I'm frozen between mother and daughter. Mother who can throw me out of the house for good, daughter whom I want to fight alongside until these people take her seriously.

"Jax," Miriam says, and tilts her head towards the door.

I shoot Essie a look, apology written across my features. She twists her mouth into a smile in acknowledgement and I head for the door, trying not to run as I grab my jacket and close the front door behind me.

Chapter Twenty-Three

ESSIE

I CAN'T BELIEVE Mum kicked Jax out. I know it isn't forever, only for the duration of this argument, but I still can't believe she did it.

I also can't believe she keeps throwing my work in my face. If David was running his own business during his summer holidays they'd be singing his praises from the rooftops, telling everyone who would listen about how amazing he is.

But it's not David. It's me. Me, working my butt off to get work done while also achieving at school during the year, then sinking every minute I can into it during weekends and holidays. Me, giving up hanging out with friends to go to markets. Me, saving every single cent to spend on fabric – and now a service on my machine.

It doesn't matter what I do. It'll never be good enough.

I continue to stack my piles of half-constructed garments into my baskets. I've been batch sewing, completing one step on all the garments at the same time, then moving on to the next step. I'm in the process of sewing thirty dresses and the space in my room really isn't big enough. It used to work in the office, but that's off limits while Jax is in residence.

Something warms in my chest as my thoughts centre on him. I've enjoyed being in his company the past few days. Even if we aren't talking, being in his presence is pleasant. He doesn't even smirk at me anymore – well, not often anyway. And these days it's more endearing than mocking.

I even got to laugh at him today when I glanced up to find him moving about the kitchen, humming and clearly dancing. Not that he'd ever admit that's what he was doing.

"Essie," Mum says, but I don't turn around. I continue tidying away my work. "Estella," she says again, her voice snappish, and this time I stop packing up, turning to face her.

"I'm trying to clean up my *hobby* so you don't have to deal with it," I snap back, voice bitter, but tears are already burning at my eyes.

"And the job? Was there even an interview?"

The question hits hard, like a punch to the face. "Of course there was," I yell, my voice beginning to crack. I hate it. I hate that I'm shaking and yelling. I want to be calm and rational and explain to her what happened, explain to her that this isn't just a hobby, that it's more than that. That I'm not just sewing a dress or two for pocket money. I have a whole accounting system, pricing tables to make sure I'm covering my costs and time. I have a contract with a shop that wants to stock and sell my items. But I never get the chance to say all that, not that anyone actually listens to what I want around here.

"And what happened? Where was it?"

"It was at the fabric shop," I say, and Mum scoffs, muttering something inaudible under her breath.

"You said a job. You didn't specify what or where," I say.

"But you didn't get it, did you?"

"No," I say, dropping my voice, trying for that calmness that I can use to explain how I got something so much better.

I take a deep breath, but before I have the chance to explain she speaks again. "I know you like all this," she says, gesturing to me and I know she means my clothes and my hair and makeup. I'm not even wearing anything interesting today, just a t-shirt and shorts, my hair piled on my head in a bun. I didn't even bother with a full face of makeup – only some eyeliner, mascara and lipstick. But it's bright pink lipstick she always seems to frown at.

"But for certain jobs, especially retail, you need to tone it down a bit. Dress appropriately."

I seethe.

There's a snort behind me and I realise David has arrived home. He steps into the kitchen. "Still no job, Essie?" He says, voice sarcastic and mocking. I hate him.

"It's none of your business," I bite out. I turn back to Mum. "I know how to dress for an interview," I say, and she gives me a look as though she doesn't believe me, as though she thinks I'm so completely useless I don't know how to get by in the real world. And maybe I don't. I don't know about a full-time job or buying food, but I have a business and no one in this family gives me the chance.

"She won't want a job now, anyway." David turns to Mum. "She won't have time because she'll be too busy making out with her new boyfriend."

I blink at him, speechless, as silence falls in the room.

"What?" I say, voice suddenly raspy.

"I heard about you and Jeremy. If you're going to date one of my friends, obviously I'm going to hear about it."

"I'm not—"

But he cuts me off, talking right over me as if I haven't said anything. "I don't know why you picked him, though." A shrug. "But at least it isn't Jax, I suppose." David laughs a little and strides from the room. If I could throw my sewing machine it would be sailing through the air right now, aimed at the back of his head.

"A boyfriend?" Mum says, her voice low. Oh God, here we go.

"No boyfriend," I say to her. "We've hung out a couple of times, but he's not my boyfriend."

"You need to be careful," she says.

"I know how to look after myself. I'm not a child."

"But you are a child. And you're behaving like a very spoilt one. We're trying to help you. A job will help your future. A boyfriend won't. Not at this point in your life."

"Right," I say, knowing it's useless. She won't listen to me, she won't hear me.

I finish packing everything into my basket. "I'll get this out of the way," I say, picking it up and heading for the stairs. I dump it in my room and return for the sewing machine. I clear every scrap of fabric from the table, from the floor.

When I return downstairs, pulling a soft, cosy hoodie over my head, Mum is setting the table with the food Jax has prepared.

"I've been thinking about this boy," she says as I pause in the doorway.

"There's nothing to think about," I say. "I'm going out for a bit."

"No, you're going to listen to me." Her eyes flash dangerously and I hesitate. "I've been thinking about this boy, and I don't think you should be seeing him. Not only is a boyfriend at your age distracting, the fact that he's older is inappropriate."

I gape at her. She didn't even bother to find out who he was, or what is really going on. Her dismissive tone slices at my heart with every word she speaks. Eventually I find some words of my own. "Is that all?"

"Yes," she says after a moment to think.

"All right, well, I'm going for a drive. I'll eat later."

"You can eat dinner with us, Estella." The way she says my name is harsh, not the soft roll I've come to expect – to enjoy – from Jax.

I turn and swipe the car keys from the hook, slamming the door behind me as I finally let the tears free.

Chapter Twenty-Four

JAX

THE SAND SHIFTS and a warm body lands next to me.

I've been sitting here, knees pulled up to my chest, arms wrapped around them, staring at the waves crashing against the shore for seconds, minutes, hours. I'm not really sure.

All I remember is the look on Miriam's face when she asked me to leave.

It shouldn't hurt. They're a family and that was obviously a family matter. I am not part of the family, no matter how long I crash in the spare room.

"I'm really embarrassed you saw that," Essie murmurs, voice barely audible over the pounding surf.

I turn towards her. She's staring at the waves now, or way out on the horizon where a container ship slips past. The sun is sinking to the horizon behind us and it's outlining Essie in gold.

There's tear tracks on her cheeks and smudges of makeup under her eyes, stray wisps of hair falling from a bun and being blown into her eyes by the sea breeze. She doesn't bother to push them away or wipe off the smudges.

My hands itch to do it, to feel how soft the skin of her

cheek is. But I made that stupid promise to her and she'll never let me hear the end of it if I break it. And I don't want to break a promise to her, even a completely stupid one like that.

"Don't be," I say, my voice matching hers. "I like you feisty."

Essie snorts but from the corner of my eye I see a smile fight its way through. It feels good to make her laugh, even in these miserable circumstances.

I was so mad when I drove out here, but as I've sat on the beach with the surf pounding against the sand I've descended into melancholy.

We sit in easy, if glum, silence, watching the evening sky change colour.

"I know that fight must have sucked," I say eventually, "but Estella, at least you have someone who cares enough about you to fight with you. Your parents obviously love you." My voice cracks on the word 'love' and a wave of embarrassment sweeps over me.

I'd prefer an actual wave to crash over my head at this point, especially when a tear tracks its way down my face.

Her hand lands on my arm, her palm hot even through the leather of my jacket. My heart almost stops. "Jackson," she whispers. "Are you *crying*?"

I swipe away the tear, but another one spills down my other cheek. "No," I croak. "Don't be ridiculous, Estella."

"Are you okay?"

"Of course," I say, managing to make the words come a little easier this time. "You're being dramatic, Estella."

Her hand disappears and I see her flinch at the word. Not at her name; she doesn't flinch when I call her Estella anymore. She doesn't snarl and snap either. In fact, I swear when those

'I's roll off my tongue these days she's trying to suppress a smile.

But the D word. Dramatic. I close my eyes, regret at my choice of word flooding me, even if I used it to poke fun at myself.

Immediately there's a distance between us. One we were finally managing to close.

"Ess," I start, but she turns her chin away, looking off down the beach. "Estella," I try again, and her face turns back towards me. "I'm sorry. Poor choice of words."

A tilt of her head; an acknowledgement and acceptance of my apology.

I release a gusting breath of a sigh and am hit with another wall of shame as two more tears leak out of my eyes.

"Jackson," she says, using the tips of her fingers on my chin to turn my face to hers. Her eyes are wide and so vividly green, the silver and black smudgy makeup enhancing the colour.

She gently cups my jaw between her palms and uses her thumbs to wipe away the tears. The pads of her thumbs are soft and smooth against the rough stubble already shadowing my jaw. I might pass out from the utter joy of finally having her skin touching mine. I breathe in deeply and try not to nestle my face into her palm. I barely manage to succeed. She smells like she always does, that indiscernible edible scent. It contrasts with the fresh tang of the ocean and I manage to suppress the urge to inhale it.

"In my admittedly limited experience," she says, and I hang on every word, "crying doesn't usually quantify being okay."

"Maybe they're happy tears," I say, again giving her an

opening to taunt me, to go back to how we've always been, to get away from this softness.

"Are they happy tears, Jackson?"

The way she's saying my name, over and over, the name that no one calls me anymore. I wonder if this is how she feels when I call her Estella. If it is I'll call her Estella every time, because it feels amazing: the little tightness in my gut. Between that and her fingertips still gently brushing my jaw I'm surprised I can see straight.

"No," I whisper.

She holds my gaze for a moment and bites her lip. I really consider giving in to my usual urge to free it from her teeth, but just because she's touching me doesn't mean she wants me to touch her. And I'm being a stubborn idiot about this stupid vow.

She drops her hands from my face. My breath catches. Is this the point where she turns it around on me? Was she luring me into some kind of trap and she's now going to use this against me forever? The little twist in my gut turns to a ripping, stabbing sensation.

Until her head lands on my shoulder. She presses our arms together, her soft green hoodie against my worn black leather and her knee falls against mine.

"Why, Jackson?"

"It doesn't matter."

"Yes it does. Tell me why … please?"

The "please" does it. I release another breath and steel my voice. "Because I'm painfully, awfully jealous of your family," I breathe against her hair.

"Of my family?" Her tone is sceptical, and I expect her to

pull away to throw me a look of disbelief. But she doesn't, and I'm relieved beyond measure.

"Yeah," I say. "I know you've all had a screaming match today. But Estella," I haul in another breath, "I don't have anyone to fight with. No one stays around long enough to fight with me. No one cares enough."

She's silent for a beat, for two.

"Do you mean your mum?"

"Yeah. The second my foot was out the door and I was mostly self-reliant, she took off to live the life I'd stopped her having. And my dad. He pissed off before I was even born. Decided he was too young to be a dad. I don't know what Mum and I would have done without Aunt Kate. But I also mean Annie. And every other girl I've ever dated."

"All those girls whose hearts you've broken?" she asks, her voice teasing, and I want to throw up. A couple more tears slip out. One drips into Essie's hair. The mortification increases the urge to vomit ten-fold.

I laugh bitterly. "Estella, all those girls … every single one of them dumped me."

Chapter Twenty-Five

ESSIE

THE WORDS HIT me like a bucket of water to the face.

There's something wrong here. How has Jax got himself such a reputation as a heartbreaker if he's been the one getting dumped every time?

I've seen a couple of girls after their Jax breakup, sitting in a huddle of other girls with mascara streaks on their faces as they sobbed over him.

I pull my head off his shoulder and turn myself in the sand so I'm facing him. Immediately I miss the contact. I miss the feel of my head resting on his shoulder, me leaning against him. I miss the feel of his face in my hands and that brief moment when I thought he was leaning into my palm.

"But …" I start but I can't put everything I want to say into words, so I settle for the most stupid response. "What?"

He huffs out a little laugh as he stares at the ocean, which is beginning to spark and shimmer with the sun sliding to the horizon behind us. The sunset light picks up golden strands in his hair, making them glow, and I wonder how I've never noticed before how beautiful it is. His lips twist into a semblance of a smile, but it's bitter. "I'm only around for a good time Estella, not a long time."

I open my mouth, close it again, bite my lip. How did we get here? When I saw his car in the carpark I was hit by this little wave of pleasure, relief that I wasn't going to be alone after the parental fallout.

I want to talk to him when it's only us and no one else is around to barge in or interrupt. Things have been so lovely between us recently and I constantly find myself wanting to seek him out and be in his presence.

But to find him sitting this way, curled in on himself, was startling. And then the tears. He wasn't full-on crying; there was no sobbing, no shaking, only a crack and waver in his voice and those few loose tears. I can tell he's mortified every time one falls.

"This girl … Annie," I say eventually. "What'd she do to you?"

Jax shakes his head then drops it to rest against his arms. "We don't have to do this, Estella," he mutters.

"I kind of think we do, Jackson," I say, relishing the way his name feels on my tongue. It gives me a little thrill every time I use it and I get a similar thrill whenever he says my name, which I've noticed has been a lot recently, and it seems to have lost its sarcastic edge.

He lifts his face, lying his head on its side across his arms so he can look up at me. His eyes are clear hazel with flecks of tawny brown, gold and green. Paired with his brown hair currently lit with sunset glow, he reminds me of a golden lion.

He meets my gaze and my heart stutters. He's looked at me before. A lot. We've made a lot of eye contact over the dinner table the past few weeks. There was the time outside my bedroom and at Melissa's party and many, many others.

But this moment feels different.

It feels momentous.

I'm discovering a side to Jax I never knew existed. I suspected he wasn't everything his reputation led us all to believe, because he's never acted like that. I've never seen him act like a heartbreaker or a sleazy flirt. Definitely not in the past few weeks, anyway, when all he's done is work, study, cook and help me.

"You're not going to give this up, are you?"

I shake my head. I place my hand on his arm, at once relieved for the layer of soft leather stopping my skin touching his and resentful of it. His eyes flick to where my purple polished fingers curl around his bicep. "Stubborn is one of the key words used to describe me," I say, and am gratified when he cracks a tiny, but real, smile. "Do you have someone else to do this with?"

His eyes close for a brief moment. "No, Estella," he says, voice weary. "The only people I have are my best friend who honestly, I'm not sure I even like that much anymore, and his parents, who let me sleep on their couch." A pause. His eyes flicker open and meet mine again. "And you, Estella."

My heart hurts. There has to be more. I can't be the only person for him. I realise I'm not.

"And Cayley and Melissa and Kate," I say quietly, and he acknowledges the statement with a tilt of his chin.

"Yeah, but they've done so much for me. I can't keep dumping stuff on them, too. I don't even need to dump it on you. Don't worry about it."

I shake my head, not accepting this. "I am going to worry

about it, Jackson. I'm going to worry about you." I squeeze his arm and try not to think about the hard muscle under his layers of clothes. "What happened with Annie?"

I twist in the sand again so I'm not staring directly at his face. I settle myself beside him, even closer than before, curled in against him. My head nestles against his shoulder.

He tenses for a second then relaxes, tilting his head to rest against mine. For a brief moment, it's perfection. The scent of him, tinged slightly with butter and garlic and whatever else he used to cook dinner, and the warmth of him swirl through my body, the latter fending off the chill of the rapidly cooling evening.

Jax lets out a long breath that's a little shaky. "Annie's the first girl I've actually broken up with," he says eventually.

I fight the desire to lift my head and stare at him. I stay as still as possible and say nothing, which is harder than I expected.

"She … I … I came home early from a mate's party … she was supposed to come with me but told me she wasn't feeling well. So I'd gone alone. It wasn't the same though, and I left early."

I suck in a breath. I have a sinking sensation, somehow knowing how this story ends. I don't quite know how it's going to get there and Jax is struggling with the words.

"I was living with a bunch of other guys. Friends of a guy from work. When I got home Annie was there, coming out of the shower. I met her in the hallway and she tried to play it off like she'd come to see me. But she barely visited when I was there. She never used our bathroom because honestly, it was gross." Another long, heavy breath. "And her clothes were in my flatmate's room."

I gasp, white hot rage curling in my belly. "No," I say.

He lifts his head from where it rests against mine and drops it between his knees again. "Yup."

"She was cheating?"

"Yup." His voice is muffled, face buried in his arms. He lifts his head and turns to look at me. "And then she thought we'd carry on as usual, even after her denials ran out and she admitted to it."

"No! Why?"

He shrugs. "But after that I couldn't even look at my flatmate. I wanted to punch him every time I laid eyes on him. After I told Annie there was no way we were staying together she started hanging out with him more and more. Right in front of my face."

I make an inelegant noise and Jax breathes a little laugh. "And that's why you had to move out? And in with us?" I say. They're not really questions. I already know the answers. We sit for a while, watching as the tide creeps closer to us, the waves crashing and rolling closer and closer each time. "I don't understand."

"Understand what?" Jax says, half turning his face towards me again, and I'm struck by the way the dying sunlight caresses his cheek and the solid line of his jaw.

"Why she would do it."

"Because I'm not good enough," he says, turning away, his voice so soft I'm not sure he means for me to hear. "I'm not worth the long term."

I slide my hand over his where it's braced across his knees and slip my fingers between his. Jax drops his gaze to where our hands twine together. My heart's pounding and I'm not sure what I'm doing but as his fingers tangle with mine, clinging on like a lifeline, I know it's the right thing.

It also feels really, really amazing.

My brain flashes back to Jeremy and the night we held hands on this beach. But tonight, with Jax, it's different.

"That's not true," I say, and he lifts his gaze, those tawny, golden eyes meeting mine. "She's wrong. Whoever else made you feel that way, they're wrong." I take a deep breath. I'm all in. "Jackson, you're lovely."

He snorts and his gaze dips away again, like he doesn't believe me, like he refuses to acknowledge what I've said. And maybe right in this moment he doesn't believe it. But I'll make him. Not today probably, but one day I'll make him believe it.

I tug at his fingers. "Come on," I say, pushing myself off the sand. I pull again at our tangled hands.

"What?" he asks, staring up at me, confusion written across his brow and my abrupt change in demeanour.

"I didn't come all this way to not have a swim."

A laugh bursts out of him and the sound is so unexpected I startle, then grin down at him. "It'll be freezing."

"So? Are you chicken, Jackson? Can't handle a bit of cold water?" I slip my fingers from his, immediately missing the comfort of his warm grasp, and peel my hoodie off over my head.

"Estella, what are you going to swim in?" he asks, his voice incredulous as though I'm suggesting something scandalous.

I roll my eyes and reach for the hem of the loose t-shirt I'm wearing. A second later I'm in a sports crop top and athletic shorts, entirely suitable swimming attire. "This," I say. "Now come on." I grab his hand again and tug petulantly. "Don't be a spoilsport."

He grins and lets me pull him to his feet, then shucks off his leather jacket and the t-shirt underneath. I avert my gaze lest he catches me staring. Because I would. Even the view from the corner of my eye almost makes me swoon.

He reaches for the button on his jeans and I realise what I've got myself in for. Thoughts of what lies beneath those jeans spiral into my brain as I turn and sprint away, running for the water. Running away from Jax, who's currently taking off his pants.

I race down the beach with the intention of running straight in and diving under, like I'm strong and fearless and the water isn't freezing like Jax predicted.

Of course, the water is freezing like Jax predicted and I shriek as I splash into it.

A moment later Jax is beside me, hissing through his teeth at the cold. I refuse to look at him. I don't want to know what he's wearing right now. I can't even think about his thighs, let alone anything else.

"Come on, Estella," he says, his voice challenging. "This was your idea, after all." He wades out further, still hissing with every breath, with every inch of skin the water engulfs. I can see him in my periphery, but I don't let myself fully look until he's waist deep in the water and the only parts of him still exposed are the parts I've already seen.

I suck in a deep breath and force myself forwards. I reach Jax's side and he gives me a sardonic grin – one I used to hate back when I thought he was always mocking me. Maybe he was, but it doesn't feel like it anymore.

"You don't have to swim, Jackson. It it's too cold for you," I say, and he laughs.

"Neither do you, Estella."

Another deep breath and I throw myself forward, plunging into the chilly water. The sun barely peeks over the horizon and the water is losing the last of its sunset glimmer. My breaths come short and sharp for a few moments while Jax stands watching me.

"Come on," I say, trying to prevent my teeth chattering. "We haven't got all day."

He laughs again, like he wasn't crying on my shoulder barely ten minutes ago. Then he plunges into the water, completely submerging himself. He surfaces, tosses his head back, shaking the hair out of his eyes, and shouts a litany of curse words into the sky where the first star has just appeared.

Chapter Twenty-Six

JAX

I PULL into the driveway behind Essie and park.

She climbs out of her car, lower half wrapped in a towel she had stashed in the boot. Her top half is wrapped in my jacket.

We stayed in the water for as long as we could both endure it. Essie's lips were turning blue and her teeth chattering when I finally called an end to it, because she never would. We'd have been like Jack from *Titanic* before she admitted defeat.

After I called an end to our impromptu swim, and Essie mocked me for it, we raced up the beach, gathering our pile of clothes and rushing to Essie's car, where she pulled out the towels.

We dried off, laughing through the shivering, and when I leaned against my car and stared at the sky, the last of the sun long vanished below the horizon, Essie leaned next to me, close enough that I could still feel her shivering. I reached for my jacket and draped it around her shoulders and she didn't argue. She slipped her arms into the sleeves, pulling it tight around her, without ever taking her eyes off my face.

Of all the times I've thought she was beautiful, this was the one I knew would be burned in my memory forever.

"We'd better get home," I whispered.

"I know," she replied, her mouth turning down at the corners, and without further words slid into her car and left. I followed right behind her all the way back.

Now she pauses beside my car again, popping her hip and leaning against the bonnet. She's still wearing my jacket. The sleeves are too long and the shoulders too broad. She looks damn good in it.

She's stopped shivering and the colour in her cheeks has lost the blue tinge. I cranked my heater the whole way and am feeling pretty toasty myself by this point. I climb out of my car and lean next to her.

"Jackson, what are you doing on Christmas?"

Her question catches me off guard. I haven't thought about Christmas. Well, I have, but each time it bubbles to the surface of my mind I bury it again, under piles of other things I have to worry about. It's only a few days away now, though. "I don't know," I say, voice hesitant, not sure where she's going with this.

"You can spend it here, you know. In case no one's told you yet. You can spend it here." She fiddles with the zipper on my jacket, eyes lowered like she's unsure how I'll react. Like she's nervous.

I step close to her and for the briefest moment angle my head to rest against hers. "Thanks, Estella. And thank you for everything tonight."

She looks up then, eyes meeting mine, face mere inches away. Her hand comes to rest against my cheek, the touch light and sweet. "You're not alone, okay? Don't forget that."

And before I even have a chance to think about kissing her and all the ways it would be a truly terrible idea, she slips away from me, heading for the house.

When I walk into the kitchen after work the next day, it looks like a bomb has gone off.

"What are you doing?" I ask Essie as she freezes in the midst of the chaos, flour streaking down one side of her face. The countertops are strewn with ingredients, broken eggshells, smears of chocolate, flour coating everything.

Essie visibly deflates, dumps the mixing bowl in her hands onto the bench and brushes loose strands of hair back out of her face, dusting them with flour. "I'm trying to bake … 'trying' being the keyword."

I survey the damage and notice a batch of sad-looking muffins already cooling on the bench. I try really hard not to smile at the state of Essie, with her rumpled apron covering her denim shorts and tank top, flour all over her, standing in the middle of this disaster zone. I try. And I fail.

"Oh, go away." She glares at me, but there's a sparkle in her eye that tells me she's definitely laughing at herself too.

"Give me a couple of minutes Estella, and I'll help you."

She exhales heavily. "Please."

"Someone has to rescue the kitchen," I say with a little laugh, and she contemplates the mess, wincing slightly.

"I'll, um, clean that up while you do your thing."

When I arrive back in the kitchen less than ten minutes later after another record-quick shower, the place almost looks like the hurricane that is Essie was never there. Essie herself is still a mess but at least we have somewhere to work now.

"What are we making?" I ask, pulling the recipe book that's propped open towards me. "A brownie?" I turn to her, one eyebrow raised. "You made this much mess trying to make a brownie?"

"And the muffins." She points feebly to the sad little lumps.

"Muffins, you say?" I ask, smirking.

"Muffins," she confirms, reaching out to whack my arm.

"Ah yes, cannot forget the muffins," I say sardonically. Her eyes flash a little with that temper that hasn't been directed my way in quite some time.

"Are you going to help me, or mock me?"

"I plan to do both, Estella," I say, leaning towards her, reaching for the mixing bowl. "Where are we up to?"

She shows me what she's done and the stage of the recipe we're up to, explains that she's sure she did everything right with the muffins but they still came out flat.

"How many times did you open the oven?"

"Well, I had to see if they were ready." She pouts a little. The flour on her temple is like a magnet for my fingers but I manage to lock them down.

"Oh, Estella, you have much to learn," I say, laughing.

"I can sew, okay? Not bake. You can't expect me to be perfect at everything."

"Perfect, no, but somewhat capable might be nice." She scowls and I laugh again. "Here." I pour the wet ingredients into the bowl with the flour and other dry ingredients. "Now, gently fold them together." She starts mixing and I hold up my hand. "Wait, you don't know what I mean, do you? I said gently."

She lets out a breath and sags a little, then looks up at me with defeated eyes. "I've got no clue," she says, despondent.

"Like this." I lift my hands, ready to take her wrists and show her how to carefully combine the ingredients. One fingertip brushes against her skin, sparks firing in my bloodstream, and I freeze as she sucks in a breath. "Do you want me to?" I ask, eyes meeting hers over the mixing bowl.

She exhales a shaky breath. "Yes," she says. A pause, then she whispers, "One hundred percent yes."

With her words, with the acknowledgement of that stupid promise I made weeks ago, something inside me crumbles and falls. Instead of my hand taking her wrist, I find it beside her cheek. My thumb traces the streak of flour, brushing it gently away from the soft, smooth skin that's better than anything I could ever have imagined.

She's watching me with those vivid green eyes, the soft pink curve of her lips parted slightly. No lipstick today. She sucks in another breath and her eyes flutter closed as she tilts her head, settling her cheek fully into my palm with a little sigh that sounds a lot like happiness.

With my free hand I take the bowl from her, placing it on the bench beside us and stepping closer. "Estella," I murmur. It's an endearment and a question.

Her voice is a whisper, but it's clear enough, sliding beneath my skin, burrowing into my bones, making me both burn and shiver. "One hundred percent," she says, meeting my eyes once more.

Chapter Twenty-Seven

ESSIE

JAX'S HAND is on my face.

He's touching me.

I might pass out on the spot because it is everything I dreamed it would be and more.

It drove me crazy yesterday when the whole time we were at the beach he wouldn't touch me, despite me touching him over and over. I kept seeing his hand move, like he was going to, or he wanted to, but he never did.

I'd forgotten about what he said to me that night of Melissa's party.

I'm not going to put my hands on you, Estella, not unless I'm one hundred percent sure that you want me to.

It wasn't until his eyes met mine over the mixing bowl, his fingertip barely brushing the skin of my wrist, and he asked me if I wanted him to, that I remembered.

I thought he was being a jerk back then. I thought that was his whole personality. I thought there was absolutely no way on this earth or any other that the moment would come when I'd actually want him to.

And now here we are and it's like there's nothing else I want more in the world than to feel his touch.

His thumb brushes against my cheek as his palm settles against my skin.

"You've got some flour," he murmurs and somehow steps even closer.

I feel heat staining my cheeks. Total disaster in the kitchen. Let's hope he never asks what possessed me to start baking in the first place.

"Can sew, not bake," I breathe, and my stomach flips as his lips curl into that smirk I once despised and now … now I love it.

His other hand settles on my waist, solid and warm.

I don't know what to do with my hands. I have too many of them and they're clumsy and in the way. I don't know where to put them.

His body is flush with mine. Not pressing, not crowding, but right there beside me, as close as can be.

Jax's hazel eyes have gone dark at the proximity. His face is so close to mine I can make out every detail; every eyelash, the tiny scar above his right eyebrow, every freckle across his cheeks. They're adorable, which is a word I never thought I'd use about Jax.

This whole thing is happening in such super slow motion, as though Jax is waiting for me to bail, to run screaming from the room.

"One hundred percent, Jackson," I breathe again, the words barely audible in the space between us.

He sighs, releasing a breath and whatever tension he's been holding about my willingness to do this, and a moment later his lips brush against mine.

The touch is light, brief, then he pulls away slightly.

I find my hand curling itself into the front of his t-shirt, which I realise is the perfect shade of green for him *and* might be my new favourite colour.

I reach, and press our lips together again. It must convince him I'm truly into this, because the kiss veers dramatically away from light and brief.

His hand slides from the side of my waist to the small of my back and the one on my face moves to cup the back of my neck. He's bracing me for the kiss that's coming.

I need it. The kiss and the bracing.

His lips press to mine. My knees go weak, butterflies taking flight in my belly, my heart thundering in my ears, but it's also only a distant noise, or maybe's that Jax's heart I can hear and mine has already ceased beating.

I kiss him until I'm dizzy and when his tongue brushes my lower lip I almost stumble backward. I throw my free hand out, the one I still haven't figured out what to do with, to catch myself on the bench, despite the fact I know Jax won't let me fall.

My hand catches the mixing bowl and it clatters against the bench top, but thankfully doesn't spill, or fall.

Jax breaks the kiss, pressing his forehead against mine, breathing heavily. He closes his eyes briefly. "That really should go in the oven or it'll be inedible too," he pants into the inch of air between our mouths.

I reach for the bowl and shove it at him. "Do it fast then."

He laughs. The sound is loud and bright. I question how I ever hated the sound of it.

I hoist myself up to sit on the edge of the counter while Jax quickly but gently mixes the batter and pours it into the tin I've already prepared. He did inspect it first to make sure I'd done it right, but accepted it. He slides the tin into the oven and sets the timer, then steps close to me again.

"You know, generally when you ask someone to help you," he says, smirking at me again, voice husky, "it means you actually do it, and that person only assists. Not that the person does everything."

"Did you really want to take all that time to teach me how to do it?" I say, voice low. The curl of his lips lets me know he gets my meaning.

He stops at the edge of the bench, in the space between my knees, and it leaves me looking down at him. He tilts his chin up to meet my eyes and his hands fall to my hips, hesitating before they land on me. I give a quick nod and they settle.

"I should really clean this up, before everyone gets home," I say, tearing my eyes away from Jax's to survey the mess around us.

"We'll tell them it was me," he says, voice low and a little rough.

I lift my hands, placing them hesitantly on his shoulders. He gusts out a little sigh and his eyes flutter closed for a second, so I leave them where they are. "No one is going to believe you made this mess," I say, my thumb brushing the edge of his t-shirt collar, barely grazing the bare skin there.

He can only reach as far as my shoulder and his head rests there, turning into my neck. His breath is hot, but leaves shivers in its wake.

"Mmhmm, but no one's going to believe you were baking of your own free will either," he says against my skin.

I laugh and I'm surprised by it. This doesn't seem like a

laughing kind of moment. This seems like a moment when I should be cute and sweet and sexy. Not guffawing.

Jax lifts his head from my neck and I expect him to pull away, to drop his hands from my hips and turn away.

He doesn't, though. "God, I love your laugh," he says instead and stretches up to meet my mouth again.

We pull apart, minutes or hours later, and spend a moment simply staring at each other, tracing the lines of each other's faces with our fingertips. I start hesitantly, my thumb creeping up the length of Jax's neck to press against the corner of his jaw, to run down the length of it.

Jax has no such hesitation as he traces the arch of my eyebrow, the curve of my lip, the length of my nose.

"How much time does that brownie have?" I ask, my voice turned raspy.

Jax glances around then back to me, leaning in to press a kiss against the pulse point in my neck. "About fifteen minutes," he says into my skin.

I push him back gently then slide off the bench, winding our fingers together as I do, gently tugging. I head for the hallway, the one that leads to the room he's staying in, but he doesn't follow. He tugs me back and pulls me right into the circle of his arms, which he slides around me, hands resting on my lower back.

"Estella," he says, and I know by the tone I've done something wrong. I was too much again. I'm just his friend's little sister after all. A distraction from his loneliness. My face burns and I can't look at him anymore. I study a spot on the bench beside me instead. "Hey," he says. "Look at me, Es." I try not to flinch at the super-shortened version of my name. I lift my gaze but stare over his shoulder, still unable to look him in the eye.

He drops his head and presses it against mine. It's my new favourite way to exist, with Jax's forehead to mine, sharing breath, our faces close enough to count eyelashes and freckles.

"Come back to me, Estella," he whispers.

He presses a quick kiss to my mouth. My hands find their way to his hips and when they make contact with the denim of his jeans he kisses me again, and again, until I'm lost in the moment, the horror and shame at my forwardness dissolving with each second he's showing me he's still into this, into me.

After another timeless bout of kissing we pause again, Jax pulling me in against his chest, my head nestling beneath his chin like the space was made for it. He speaks, voice low, and I feel the vibrations as much as I hear the words. "We should probably ta—"

He's cut off by a knock at the door.

Oh my God.

I shove away from him right as he hurriedly takes three steps back. We stare at each other across the kitchen.

What the hell have we been doing? My family could have come home at any point. David could have come home at any point.

And Jax? I was making out with *Jax* in my kitchen?

He clears his throat. "You going to get that? I'll start cleaning up."

I nod and head for the door, voice disabled and my entire body shaking.

Making out with Jax in my kitchen?

Yes, yes I was, and I cannot bring myself to regret it. I can't even pretend I don't think he wanted it as much, if not more, than I did, with the way he responded every time I touched him.

I smile as my heart lifts.

I definitely don't hate Jax anymore. I haven't for a while. And today's events indicate that it's gone a lot further than not hating him.

I remember the words he was saying when the knock interrupted us. *We should probably talk.*

I wonder what was coming next. I don't mind talking, but what I really want to do is kiss him again.

I swing open the front door and find a girl standing there. She's tiny with long, icy-blonde hair, wearing a super-soft sage green t-shirt and white denim shorts. She looks like she's stepped straight off a Pinterest board.

"Hi," she says, voice melodic and sweet. "Is Jax here?"

Chapter Twenty-Eight

JAX

I DROP the bowl and swear loudly when it bounces off my bare foot.

I was rinsing it in the sink when Essie walked back into the room. I smiled at her, still dusted in flour and looking decidedly rumpled.

Her cheeks were flushed and mine probably matched. My heart was skipping in my chest. Actually skipping.

Not only had Essie let me touch her, she let me kiss her. And she kissed me back.

And what a kiss it was. What kisses they were, because that was far, far more than one kiss.

I could have been lost in her for hours, learning the curves of her, the taste and smell of her.

We need to talk about what happened, about what's going to happen next, and I'm weirdly looking forward to it, *especially* if it means I get to kiss her some more.

Then Essie steps aside and the bowl hits my foot, bouncing across the room with a weird clanging noise. *At least it doesn't break,* I think.

Out of the corner of my eye I catch Essie starting forward, but the other girl beats her to it and sweeps me into an embrace, wrapping her arms around my waist, pressing herself into my chest.

"Oh, Jaxy, are you okay?" Her voice is soft and sweet in my ear.

I manage to speak, my voice a hoarse croak. "Annie."

I try to untangle myself from her, from this hug that feels far less about me than her. I catch the scent of her perfume and the smell is so familiar it makes my world tilt.

Glancing up, I catch sight of Essie, still standing frozen in the doorway. The smile, the spark in her eyes that was there moments ago is gone. Her face is set and cold as she watches us.

"I need to clean up," she says, voice wooden.

I nod, manage to get free of Annie's grasp long enough to reach for the bowl I dropped. My foot is throbbing but it really seems like the smallest of my issues right now. "I'll help."

Essie strides forward and plucks the bowl right out of my hands. "I think you have something else that requires your attention." Her voice is tight, her body rigid with tension as she stacks dirty dishes beside the sink, then slams containers of ingredients back into the pantry.

"Estella." I reach for her, my hand about to make contact with the skin of her arm when she shakes her head.

"Zero percent, Jackson. Just go." Her words hit harder than that bowl bouncing off my foot. They hurt far, far worse too.

"I need to talk to you, Jaxy," Annie says beside me, and I startle a little. I've forgotten she's here, that she needs something. All I can think about is the look on Essie's face, the change in her voice, the stark difference between the moments before Annie arrived and after, and how I would give anything to have the Essie from before back again, to have her wrapped up in my arms hesitantly drawing the lines of my face with her fingertips. To have her back laughing, my hands on her because she wants them there as I press kisses to the silky-smooth skin of her neck.

But that Essie isn't here right now, and every second with Annie in the room is delaying that Essie's return.

But I don't know what to do with Annie.

Why is she here? What does she want?

I don't want to take her to my room because that feels callous, especially when I wouldn't take Essie there. But that's a whole other thing we need to unpack later, once I've found out what Annie wants and sent her on her way. I glance outside and remember the seat tucked under a tree in the corner of the garden. A corner that you can't see from the kitchen, so at least Essie won't have to watch whatever this conversation is going to be.

"Come on," I say, turning to Annie, my eyes lingering on Essie until the last possible moment, trying to convey everything I'm thinking and feeling to her. I lead Annie down the hall, right past my room so Essie probably thinks we're going there anyway, then out the back door. I slam it loudly, stomping across the small deck attached to the back of the house, desperate for Essie to know I didn't take Annie to my room.

Annie follows me. If she notices my weird behaviour she doesn't comment. If she noticed the tension between Essie and me she doesn't comment on that either.

I lead her to the seat and sprawl onto it, angling myself away from her so she can't get too close to any part of me except my knee. Annie perches beside me, all sweet and gentle.

"What's up?" I say, trying to start this conversation, since Annie seems more interested in fiddling with the ends of her hair than actually telling me why she turned up, potentially ruining everything.

"Was that David's little sister?"

I flinch. Rearrange myself on the seat, pushing myself even further from her. Clear my throat. "Yeah, Essie."

"You called her something else?"

I laugh, a short, cranky sort of laugh. "Yeah. I call her Estella. It grinds her gears."

"Oh," Annie says. "She's not what I expected."

I feel a surge of protectiveness towards Essie. "What is it you expected?" I try to temper my words. I'm not sure if I'm successful, or if Annie simply isn't paying that much attention.

She gives a small shrug. "I don't know." Then nothing else.

I sigh, closing my eyes and steeling myself. This was something I hated about being with Annie. I always had to be the strong one. I was always the one who had to deal with hard things, like this conversation. She came to me and yet somehow it's falling on me to make it happen. "Why are you here, Annie?"

She looks at me then, blue eyes wide. "I – I wanted to say I'm sorry." Her voice is a husky whisper. It's quavering. Because of course she's going to cry. Not that I can talk, since it was me crying twenty-four hours ago.

"I think you've already said it," I say. "Only it didn't seem very sincere when you were picking your clothes up off the floor of another guy's room." I hate myself as the words come out. Because yeah, she cheated and she ruined what we had, but I still don't like to be a jerk. Even if she does deserve it. I recall Essie's hot rage about it and hate myself a little less.

I glance back at Annie as a tear falls down her cheek. Right on cue.

"I made a horrible mistake," she says, voice still wobbling. "Jax, you have to believe me. I'm so sorry. I got all caught up and it just happened. But I never wanted to hurt you. I love you, Jaxy. And I want you to know I'm sorry, and that I want to be with you. Not with him. With you."

And there it is. What I've wanted all along.

Someone who loves me. Someone to want me enough to come back to me. Someone who thinks I'm worth enough to not simply walk away from.

She's back and she wants me to take her back.

I really, really wish she hadn't been so careless with me in the first place.

Chapter Twenty-Nine

ESSIE

I NEED to get out of here. I need to get out before Jax and Annie come back, or potentially worse, Jax comes back alone and wants to talk about what happened.

I'm not sure that's something I ever want to talk about or acknowledge even happened. Not anymore.

Right before I opened the door and that beautiful girl was standing there asking for Jax, it's all I wanted to do.

I wanted to talk to him about it, ask him what it meant, perhaps do it again. I was pretty sure he wanted to, with the way his fingers laced through my hair as he said we needed to talk about it.

Right before Annie interrupted us.

Right before the reality of our situation hit me in the face. There is no way anything can happen between Jax and me. From his glamorous ex-girlfriend (who by now might not be an ex anymore), to the fact that he's my brother's best friend.

There is no conceivable way it can work, and if we try I'm going to lose someone I suddenly care about way too much.

I wash the dishes as quickly as possible, stacking them to

dry themselves. I wipe benches and finish putting away the ingredients. I pull the brownie from the oven when the timer beeps, dumping it on the cooling rack I already had on the counter.

Then I bail. I get in my car and drive. I'm not surprised that I end up at the beach, sitting on the same patch of sand where Jax and I sat together yesterday.

Today it's me crying, which is something I don't fully understand, but huge tears roll down my cheeks in unstoppable waves regardless.

I can't even figure out if I'm upset because I kissed Jax, or because Annie is gorgeous, or because he even entertained the thought of talking to her and didn't throw her out of the house on sight.

Maybe I'm crying because I saw the look on his face when his eyes landed on her. Shock, but also this sense of longing, like he's been waiting for her to come back to him.

The way he spoke about her yesterday makes me think he has been waiting for her. Maybe he's been trying all along to reunite with her, trying to convince her to choose him, and his breakup with her was a spur of the moment thing he's regretted ever since.

Maybe tears are streaming down my cheeks because kissing him in the first place was an exceptionally bad idea, yet it was also one of the greatest moments of my life.

My skin still burns with every place he's touched me. I can feel his hands tangling in my hair, the way he pressed hot kisses against my neck, breathing me in.

I wonder how long he's wanted to do it.

Is it since the night of Melissa's party, when he told me he wouldn't put his hands on me unless he was certain I wanted it?

When he said that to me, I never thought the day would come when I'd actually want him to touch me, let alone like that. It wasn't until his finger brushed against my wrist and he paused to ask permission that I even realised how badly I wanted him to.

I sit there running my fingers through the soft sand, hoping it'll calm me, but the tears keep flowing.

I compare Jax to Jeremy and come to the horrifying conclusion that I was way more into kissing Jax. Probably because he opened up to me and I got to see that vulnerable side to him. Maybe Jeremy and I need to connect more like that. Then I might enjoy kissing him more.

The thoughts of the two boys overwhelm me.

I need to do something to get my mind off this mess. I can't sit here all night crying into the sand. For a start, it reminds me far too much of Jax sitting here crying into the sand.

I also can't go home yet, because I'm not ready to deal with the storm that is my family, with Jax in the middle of it. Tonight is not the night to sit across the dinner table from him. Annie's arrival is irrelevant to that.

If Brooke was here, that's where I'd go. But I don't know that I can randomly turn up at anyone else's house with red eyes and blotchy cheeks. And there's no one else I can talk to about Jax. It's too big of a thing to unpack with anyone else, from my anger at his intrusion on my life, to the tentative friendship we've formed, and now the kissing. I don't have it in me to go through everything.

My phone rings and I fish it out of my pocket, expecting it to be Mum summoning me home for dinner.

It's not, though. It's Cayley.

I wipe my cheeks, take a couple of deep breaths and swipe to answer.

"Hi Essie," she chirps at my rusty hello. "How are you?"

"I'm good," I say, hoping my voice doesn't give me away. I don't usually like to cover my real emotions too much, but I can hardly dump on my client about me kissing her cousin. "And you?"

"Oh great, though I don't know what Mum was thinking having this wedding right after Christmas. Everyone's going on holiday and I can't get hold of people to confirm or ask questions about anything."

I laugh. "That must be awful."

"It is," she says with a little laugh. "Anyway, I know you're probably flat out in the lead up to Christmas too, but is there any chance we can squeeze that fitting in before Christmas? If you're ready for it, of course."

"Yeah, of course. I was meaning to get in touch with you anyway and set it up. Sorry, my day got away on me," I say, cringing at myself.

I was supposed to message Cayley. I'd intended on doing it while waiting for the baking to finish and I spent that time kissing Jax instead.

Cayley brushes aside my apology and we make a time for the day before Christmas Eve. I have two days to get those dresses ready for fitting. It shouldn't be too hard. The garment is somewhat constructed. It's a matter now of getting the sizing right before finishing everything off and adding in all the final details.

At least it gives me an excuse to avoid Jax. I'll be far, far too busy.

Chapter Thirty

JAX

ESSIE IS HIDING FROM ME.

It's been three days since Annie showed her face and everything else that happened before Annie showed her face.

In that time I haven't been alone with Essie once. She's only been in the same room as me when her family is around too, and that has pretty much only been to eat dinner.

It's driving me absolutely mad.

I tripped over my own feet walking across the workshop yesterday because I was thinking about the way she smelled that day in the kitchen, like chocolate and vanilla. Her normal scent is something light and fresh. It still smells edible, whatever perfume it is she wears, but that day in the kitchen when she smelled more like the chocolate brownie she was attempting to bake … I'll never be able to smell a brownie and not think of her.

Each day when I get home from work I expect to see Essie working in the kitchen, at the counter or the table, with laptop or sketchpad or sewing machine, like she has been for the past few weeks.

But she's never there. She's in her room, the door closed, music softly filtering out.

I know she keeps her door closed because I've been up those stairs, standing outside her door every day since it happened. I've got as far as lifting my fist to tap against the door. But I've never actually been able to go through with the knocking part.

I've stood with my forehead against the door though, hoping she'll open it and I'll land flat on my face at her feet. At least she can't ignore me then.

I need her, both to tell her what happened with Annie and to talk to her about what happened between us.

I need her, because she's the only one who knows anything about either of them.

That selfishness wars constantly with the knowledge that if Essie wanted to talk about it, she would. She has no issue with telling people exactly what she thinks. Though sometimes I think my assessment of her in that regard isn't entirely accurate now. Sometimes she'll tell you exactly what she's thinking, especially if it's me she's telling, but seeing her at home, with her family, I've seen her swallow her opinions and feelings on so many occasions it makes my stomach hurt.

I miss her, though.

I miss her company, even when she's only working quietly at the table while I make dinner, or her sudden outbursts of cursing, or the way she'll sing a few lines of a song with complete commitment even though it's obvious those are the only words she knows.

I flop back onto my bed, scowling as the frame squeaks. I'm grateful for the place to stay, but this bed is wearing thin. Even the dodgy bed frame supplied for me in the flat was more comfortable than this one.

I've been home from work for fifteen minutes. I've showered, because that is the first thing I have to do every day. I'm too terrified to touch anything before I do in case I smear it with grease or grime.

And now I lie here and stare at the box in my hand. A little midnight blue gift box with a purple ribbon.

It's a Christmas present for Essie.

I got a ridiculously extravagant food hamper thing for her whole family and it's already under the Christmas tree in the lounge.

But I don't know what to do with this little box. I know I can't give it to her in front of her family, which leaves me sitting firmly in my last window of opportunity right now. We won't have the chance to be alone again before Christmas.

I take a deep breath and steel myself. I've faced down Essie before, in whatever rage she's been in. I can do it again.

I throw on a shirt, though I do briefly consider leaving it off in the hopes it will distract her from being angry at me. The thought of her on the beach the other night, barely able to look at me as I stripped off my shirt and jeans, tugs a smile from deep within.

I couldn't look at her either though, not without staring at the curve of her waist in the space between her sports bra and shorts, the prickle of goosebumps over her exposed skin or the angle of her collarbone. It's not like I haven't seen her collarbone before. Essie wears tank tops and other collarbone-revealing clothes all the time.

Thinking about her collarbone is bad, especially now I know what it feels like against my mouth. Same goes for that curve of her waist, which as I predicted is the perfect fit for my hand.

I shove away the thoughts of Essie's body and kissing Essie. The box clasped firmly in my hand, I head for the stairs.

I reach the landing right as Essie's door swings open and she steps out. She glances around and freezes when she sees me.

"Oh," she says, eyes wide. Her hair is up in two buns again, which might be my favourite way for her to wear her hair, aside from having it down so I can slide my fingers into it. I shut those thoughts down real fast.

"Hey, Estella," I say, wondering if I'll regret using her name today.

"Um, hi," she says. "Bathroom. And very busy." She turns and enters the bathroom across the hall from her room, closing the door with a solid click.

This might be harder than I thought. She's not hostile, but the avoidance is evident. I linger for a moment in the hallway, but it feels creepy waiting for her outside the bathroom. Curiosity gets the better of me and I peer into her room. She might gut me where I stand if she finds me in here, but the allure is too great. I've been playing with fire this whole time and I'm about to jump into the flames anyway. May as well do it a little earlier than planned.

Essie's room is as bright and bold as she is. And as chaotic.

There're piles of fabric in stacks across the floor, piled haphazardly in the corner and along the wall. It's all folded neatly and organised by some system I'm sure, though I can't exactly tell how the system works. The sheer volume of it, however, lends itself to mayhem.

There's a pile of paper and notebooks, pens and other

stationary on the floor beside her desk, clearly gathered up and dumped there when she needed the desk for her sewing machine.

Beside the window there's a dressing table, the top scattered with cosmetics, hair products and a wild array of knickknacks.

Photos, mostly of Essie and her friends (though a few are of celebrities in extravagant dresses), are haphazardly stuck to the walls, to the side of the dresser and along the window frame. There's a string of fairy lights tangled around the bedframe.

The most telling thing is that Essie's personal things are scattered and cluttered and chaotic. But anything to do with her business, with the sewing or the fabric, it's neat and ordered. Well, as much as it can be when she's so obviously been displaced from her usual space.

I consider the box in my hand; the way Essie is clearly avoiding me. I survey the room again, find a spot and set the box down.

A framed picture catches my eye. It's of Essie and another girl and it so perfectly captures who Essie is in one shot that I want to pick it up and take it with me.

"What're you doing in here?"

Oh, this isn't good. Essie's voice is cold and distant, back to the way it was before.

Before the kissing, before that night at the beach, before the market when I finally got her to stop hating me for a few minutes.

I was supposed to leave the gift and go, and I curse myself for lingering. "I was leaving you this," I say, picking up the box again as I turn to face her.

She looks entirely unimpressed. Her arms are crossed over

her chest and her expression is bored. Not a hint of interest or even that flash of anger I've seen so many times before. "What is it?"

I hold the box out to her but she doesn't reach for it. I contemplate taking her hand and pressing the gift into it. But I can't, because I know she most definitely doesn't want me to touch her now.

I drop the box onto her bed and step close to her, careful not to touch her, but close enough that I can lower my voice and speak softly along her temple. "It's a present. Merry Christmas, Estella," I say, then step around her and head for the door.

Chapter Thirty-One

ESSIE

I STAY FROZEN in place after Jax leaves my room, closing the door softly behind him. His words slide along my skin and nestle in deep somewhere. Probably in my traitorous heart. It's not so much the words he said, but the way he said them. They carry so much *weight*. Everything he says seems to.

I stare at the little blue box with the purple ribbon he's dropped onto the end of my bed. I wonder if he knows that shade of purple is my favourite, or if it's a total coincidence. I honestly don't know which I'd prefer: that he knows me that well, or that it happened by chance.

I should go and talk to him. I should open this present then thank him for it. I should ask him about what happened with Annie, what happened between *us*.

But as usual, whenever thoughts of Annie creep into my mind, I lose all sense. All I can see is the look on Jax's face when she walked into the kitchen – that mixture of surprise and longing – and the way her hand landed on his cheek as she rushed to him, his eyes fluttering closed at the contact.

In any other situation, if his ex-girlfriend hadn't turned up, and Jax dropped a bowl on his foot, I would have laughed and mocked him relentlessly for it. He probably would have laughed with me.

Now though, I can hardly bear to be in the same room as him.

I've been hiding from him and he probably knows it, because he's been going out of his way to make eye contact with me, to ask me questions, to come up to my room and give me Christmas presents.

I really don't know what to do with that. The present itself or the fact that he gave me one.

What does it mean?

I collapse onto my bed, fingering the ribbon tying the box closed as I stare at it.

I don't want to admit the way Jax makes me feel. Sometimes I wish I could go back to the times when I hated him, when I thought he was an arrogant jerk, before I knew what it would feel like to have his hands on my body.

I stare at the box a little longer, trying to puzzle out my feelings, but there're too many and they're too tangled.

They're not only about Jax, either.

The fight with Mum is still twisting through my mind; the way she dismisses my sewing business, how she told me a boyfriend was inappropriate, especially one that's older than me.

It's like she doesn't realise I've actually grown up in ways other than simply being of an age to have a 'suitable job'.

I know she's busy, and she's always stressed. The vet clinic we own goes through ups and downs like all businesses do, and the past few months seem to have been pretty much in the down category. Mum and Dad don't talk about the business at home, or at least not when I'm around, but I think they had a couple of staff leave and it's put extra pressure on.

Plus the lead up to Christmas always seems to be more chaotic, with pets tearing into presents and eating things they shouldn't, and owners realising there'll be a couple of days when my parents won't actually be working, and deciding their pets need check-ups or booster shots.

As a result, I've barely seen Mum since the fight we had, which is fine because it's not like we're going to have a big heart-to-heart about it.

I sigh and drop the gift box onto the bed beside me, staring at the glow in the dark stars scattered across my ceiling. I should probably take them down. I'm too old for cutesy glow-in-the-dark stars. But I like them. It's not like anyone ever sees my room except Brooke, anyway.

I roll over, fully prepared to scream my feelings into my pillow, when my phone vibrates in my pocket.

I pull it out and swipe to see the text.

> **Jeremy:**
> Hey gorgeous

My heart skips a beat at the endearment, at the thought of Jeremy and his casual affection with me. With everything that's happened with Jax this week I've mostly wiped Jeremy from my mind, except for the few times he's sent me a quick text to say hello, which hasn't been very often.

> **Jeremy:**
> Any chance I can steal you away from your family tomorrow night? I know it's Christmas Eve so only if it's not a problem. I want to see your beautiful face.

My cheeks heat at his message. I reply immediately.

> **Essie:**
> Tomorrow sounds great. Family no problem. They're all working anyway.

> **Jeremy:**
> Cool. I'll pick you up about 5 when I get off work

> **Essie:**
> Sounds good. Text me when you get here. Can't wait

> **Jeremy:**
> Me either babe

I collapse back onto my bed, dropping my phone onto my chest and shifting the present from Jax to my bedside table.

This feels better.

Jeremy taking me on a date. It's better than the shifting emotions and turmoil of whatever happened between me and Jax.

I know Jeremy isn't forever, he's barely for the summer, but in some ways being with him feels easier than being with Jax.

Not that I'm *with* Jax. Or could ever be with Jax.

I push thoughts away of his lips against my neck, his hand in my hair, and refocus my thoughts on Jeremy and the date he's taking me on tomorrow.

I want to see your beautiful face.

It makes me blush again.

When my phone rings five minutes later with a FaceTime call from Brooke, my cheeks are still pink when I answer the call.

"Well, you look happy," she says by way of greeting.

I grin, my face hurting. "I've got a date tomorrow."

"Oooh, is it with Jax?" She waggles her eyebrows.

"What? No!" My blush reignites, flaring across my cheeks. I hope the call quality is poor enough that she can't notice. "With Jeremy," I say.

Her face bunches for a moment, eyebrows drawing down, mouth twisting. It clears in a second though and I wonder if it was to do with call quality. "Oh, that'll be fun."

I'm not sure about her tone. Is she being sarcastic? She almost sounds like she's faking excitement for me, but I can't figure out why.

I haven't told her about Jax. I haven't told her about the fight with Mum, or the way I ran out and found Jax sitting on the beach, both of us teary and sad.

I definitely haven't told her what we talked about, or the events of the following day, which still make my heart race. The thought of those impossible-to-repeat moments in the kitchen.

All I've told her is that maybe Jax isn't as bad as I first thought and maybe he's actually a little bit of a decent human. Only a little bit, though.

"He's so gorgeous," I say, pushing past the uncomfortable feelings I had at her response. "And so sweet. Lots of fun, too. I wonder what we're going to do."

"Tell me more about him," Brooke says, readjusting her position on her bed at her dad's house, settling in.

"Well," I start, and I tell her all about Jeremy, refusing to allow thoughts of Jax to cross my mind again.

Chapter Thirty-Two

JAX

THERE'S a knock at the door and I wipe my hands on a tea towel before going to answer it. I assume Essie's not going to hear the knocking from upstairs, not with the music she's got blasting.

I swing the door open and immediately want to slam it shut again.

Jeremy stands on the doorstep, hands buried in his jeans pockets. He's got his head dipped down so he can look through his fringe. His corny smile vanishes at the sight of me. I guess all that was for Essie.

"Hey man," he says, straightening up. "How's it going?"

"Yeah, all right," I say, managing to bite back on the anger coursing through me.

Jealousy. I hate it.

"What brings you over?" I ask, as if I don't know he's here for Essie. There's no one else here for him to be seeing. The question is, does Essie know he's here?

"I'm picking up Essie," he says, totally nonchalant, like I'm not standing here glowering at him, emanating "I want to kick your ass" vibes.

I flex my fingers, forcing them to relax from the fists they've formed of their own accord. "I'll let her know you're here," I say, voice tight.

"If you point me in the right direction, I'll find her," he says with a smug smile.

I'd like to erase it from existence.

I give him a look. "Wait here."

I take the stairs two at a time. Essie's door is open for once and she's in front of the mirror, fussing with her hair. If she'd asked me I would have told her it looked perfect. But she didn't, because she is still not speaking to me.

"Estella," I say, knocking loudly on the door frame.

She startles and spins around to face me. Lipstick, eyeliner, a really cute outfit – a purple fitted skirt and white tank top with frilly sleeve things. I look a little closer and realise it's a lacy frill. It's Essie, but it's also not, in a way. Something about it is slightly off, but I can't put my finger on it. It's almost like it isn't *Essie* enough.

Taking her in as she slides her feet into heels, something inside me crumples up.

She knew he was coming.

"Sorry, can't chat, on my way out," she says as she grabs her purse and scurries past me.

"Yeah, your ride is downstairs."

She freezes, staring at me with her mouth a soft 'o' of surprise and eyes wide. The expression barely lasts a second before it shifts and hardens, her lips twisting to the side. She's annoyed. The little part of me that crumpled up smooths out the tiniest bit.

"Estella, before you go."

She doesn't let me finish. "I don't need your warnings, Jackson."

I breathe a little sigh of relief when she calls me that. I was worried she knew how it makes me feel and was going back to calling me Jax. This version of my name is said with heavy sarcasm, but I'll take it, even if she does sound like she hates me a little again.

"I wasn't going to warn you," I say, stepping in front of her. Her eyes fall to my hands, floating in mid-air between us while I war with this stupid, overpowering desire to touch her, to feel that connection with her again. "I was going to say we need to talk about the other day."

She shakes her head. "No, we don't."

"Estella," I say, my voice catching.

She cuts me off again. "We don't need to talk about it. I don't want to talk about it, okay? Don't tell anyone it ever happened and we can pretend like it didn't."

I blink at her. She wants to pretend it didn't happen? I'm still speechless when she continues.

"David can never know. God, can you imagine how he'd react? No. It didn't happen, okay? You're off the hook." She glances towards the stairs. "I have to go. I won't be home for dinner." She gives me a tight little smile and strides from the room, the seemingly unshakeable confidence back in place. Except now I know it's not unshakeable. I know it's plenty shakeable, even if most of the time she can brush it off and laugh at herself. But if someone hits the wrong spot that confidence shakes plenty.

I hear the front door slam. I'm alone again.

I'm about to return to the kitchen to begin my usual dinner preparations when my phone buzzes with a text.

It's from Miriam, letting me know that she and Karl are working late and will grab dinner once they finish at the clinic. An animal emergency of some kind, no doubt.

I'm off the hook for dinner.

It also means I'm alone on Christmas Eve. David's on the late shift again so he won't be home for another couple of hours.

Essie's out with Jeremy. The thought makes me seethe again.

I always thought Jeremy and I were friends. Sure, we haven't been close since I left school and started working, but we still hang out in the same circles, and I've never had a problem with him before.

Not until Melissa's birthday party.

I still don't know if it's the anger at what I saw him doing, or the jealousy, but I don't think I can ever consider the guy my friend again.

I sigh and sit on the edge of Essie's bed. The gift box is sitting on her bedside table, the ribbon tied in a neat bow.

She hasn't opened it. Another punch to the gut.

Everything I feel about Essie is a lot. The feelings are always big; there's no in-between. There's "She's driving me absolutely crazy", or there's "I want nothing more in this world than to kiss her", and then there's this feeling. The feeling that is so overwhelmingly painful I don't know how to process it.

With all the girls I've dated in the past, when they eventually ended things – dumping me often in spectacular fashion complete with dramatic tears – I haven't felt much. I'm so accustomed to the loss.

Annie was a slash across my heart, and at the time I thought it was the end of everything. The heartbreak felt immeasurable. But not even that was like this thing with Essie.

Not that there is a thing with Essie, apparently. It's all in my head and it's so typical that the one girl I want more than anything is the one I can't have.

She's right, too, about David. He would absolutely flip his lid. He warned me the day I moved in, and again since, not to go near Essie. If he ever found out about me kissing her he'd kick me out in a flash and never speak to me again. I can't lose whatever friendship I have left with him, and this place is the closest thing I have to a home now. I can't give that up, not for a girl who clearly doesn't want anything to do with me.

I sigh and fall backwards onto the bed. I take a deep breath and Essie's scent hits me. That fruity perfume she wears. I realise where I am. This is so inappropriate.

I pry myself up and off the galaxy-printed duvet and leave her room, hitting the power button on her stereo as I go, plunging the room and the whole house into silence.

As I trudge down the stairs I pull out my phone and text Cayley. She's my one chance to not spend the night sitting here alone studying calculus.

She texts me back almost immediately. She'll be round in fifteen minutes, bearing food.

I grin at my phone. I need a distraction from Essie, from thoughts of her out with Jeremy, and Cayley can provide that, even if it will only be her moaning for three hours about planning her mother's wedding.

It's a different kind of pain, but I'll take it.

Chapter Thirty-Three

ESSIE

I EASE the door behind me, clicking it gently closed.

The house is quiet.

Only the glow of Christmas tree lights and the flicker of the TV with its sound turned almost all the way down light the living room.

Mum and Dad mustn't be home yet. I breathe a sigh of relief. I'm not out too late, but I really can't be bothered having to explain myself to them, to endure the looks and potential lectures I'll receive.

I don't want to spoil what was a perfectly lovely evening.

I managed to hold my tongue and not tell Jeremy off for coming to the door instead of letting me know when he'd arrived. I'm glad it was Jax who answered the door, not my parents or David. But I was still a little mad.

Jeremy was so sweet though, with his dimpled grin and the blond hair falling into his eyes.

He bought us burgers and milkshakes and we drove to the lookout overlooking town and the beach off to the left. We sat up there at a picnic table with peeling paint and ate, talking the entire time, and before he drove me home Jeremy kissed me against his car again.

The kisses were long and languid, his lips sending shivers across my skin as he pressed his body against me, the cold metal of the car at my back.

I refuse to acknowledge the thought that fired across my brain in the moment Jeremy's lips trailed down my neck. That this was different to kissing Jax.

Jax is not an option. Jeremy is.

I step into the lounge, expecting to see David sprawled across the couch watching some trash TV. It's not him, though.

In the dim light I can make out a blonde girl, her hair piled on her head in an elegant, only slightly tousled bun. Jax is lying across the couch, his head in her lap. Her arm lies across his chest and they're asleep.

I feel a pang of loneliness at the sight. They're clearly comfortable enough to fall asleep like this, cuddled together on the couch. The casual affection they share leaves me bereft.

There's also a lot of jealousy, which is a little unexpected, especially after my night with Jeremy.

Jax will barely touch me. I know why, but I still long for the casualness of his touch. When he withholds it even though I know he wants to touch me, I feel like screaming at him.

But then I messed everything up again and maybe he doesn't want to touch me anymore. Maybe it was a fleeting moment, a blip in time. Throwing Jeremy in his face probably doesn't help my situation.

I turn away, planning to head upstairs, lock myself in my room and likely cry myself to sleep. My bag bumps into the corner of the doorframe and the girl jerks awake at the noise.

She turns towards me and I expect to see the delicate features of Annie's face.

It isn't Annie though. It's Cayley.

She blinks at me for a moment, then down at Jax, still sleeping on her lap. "Hey, Essie," she says quietly. She switches off the TV and carefully manoeuvres herself out from under Jax. She settles his head on a cushion, picks up her own bag and follows me to the kitchen.

"Sorry," I say. "I didn't mean to wake you."

She laughs softly. "Probably for the best. Mum might lose her mind if I'm not home on Christmas morning." She says it with a smile though, like she knows her mum would understand and it wouldn't be a big deal.

I laugh awkwardly. I never quite know what to say to Cayley, how to act around her. "Do you want a drink or something?" I ask, as I fill the jug and switch it on.

"Ooh, do you have tea?"

I open the cabinet and gesture inside. "How many types would you like?"

She laughs again. "Do you have something fruity? Berries or something?"

I nod and pull out my favourite, showing her the box. When she nods I drop the teabags into the two prettiest mugs in the house then lean against the bench, waiting for the water to heat.

I realise I'm leaning in the same place I sat the other day when Jax stood between my knees and kissed me. I stand abruptly and shift away. I clear away the fast food containers on the bench and Cayley moves to stand from her perch at the counter. "Oh, sorry, that's my mess."

I wave her away. "Don't worry about it. Jax cooks for us

almost every night. I can clean up after him once."

She settles back on her seat. "He's such a good cook."

I nod and am relieved when the water boils and I can turn away to finish making the tea. "How come he doesn't want to do that as a job?" I'm not sure where the question came from, but now I've voiced it I really want to know.

"Well, first of all, being a chef usually requires some form of working at night. I'm not sure if you've noticed, but he's not a night person." She waves in the direction of the lounge where Jax is asleep at 9 pm.

"Cafés don't work at night," I say, and she nods.

"Which brings us to point two. I think the main reason is that he loves it and doesn't want it to be a job. He doesn't want to lose the joy of it by having to do it every day to be able to live. He likes to cook for people because it's how he shows he cares about them, or it's how he thanks people. It's like," she pauses, takes a sip of tea, "it's like his love language, you know?"

I think about the way Jax moves in the kitchen with comfort and ease, the way everything he makes is delicious, looks good, is well thought out, made with care. I remember him being adamant he didn't mind cooking for us every night.

I don't know what a love language is. But I think I understand what Cayley is saying.

"What's this, then?" I say, gesturing to the mostly empty containers. "Does he not cook for you?"

Cayley laughs. "That is my attempt at cooking for him," she says. "I'm terrible at it, even though he's tried to teach me. So I buy him food to show him I care." Her smile is so disarming. I relax, propping my hip against the counter across from her, away from the kissing spot.

"Do you think it means as much?" I cringe as soon as the words leave my mouth. "Oh, I didn't mean it like that. I don't know what I'm trying to say. Sorry." I ramble, trying to cover my awkwardness. I take a sip of tea to stop myself talking and burn my tongue. Dammit.

"It's okay, Essie, I know what you mean." She smiles. "I think a lot of the time it's okay to show someone you care about them in the ways that you can. Like I can't cook, so I don't really try, but I can organise nearly anything. So to show my mum and Travis that I care about them and their wedding, I'm organising it for them." She pauses to drink more tea as her words settle over me. "But I think there are times when it's really helpful to step outside that comfort zone, to show someone you care about them by doing something that's hard or terrifying for you. And I'm not only talking about food. What I mean is, if talking about emotions is hard for you, like it is for Jax, then when you really need to show someone you care, you have to open up to them. You need to show them the part of yourself that's most afraid. My boyfriend was the same." Another drink. "Do I make any sense?" Another light laugh and a shake of her head.

"Yeah," I say slowly, thinking of Jax and his cooking, him opening up on the beach. I think about the way I tried to bake something for him because I'd seen the pleasure it gave him to cook for someone else and I wanted to feel that – and I wanted him to know that there were people out there who'd do the same for him. All these realisations hit me at once and I don't know what to do with them, especially not now when I've so effectively screwed it all up.

But all of those things: that was each of us trying to show the other we care.

Chapter Thirty-Four

JAX

CHRISTMAS MORNING DAWNS fresh and cool. I know the heat will come later in the day, but for now I enjoy the respite.

I wake up before the time of my usual alarm. Which is typical when today would have been a great day to sleep in and one of the few opportunities I get these days.

Now I'm like a very small child who's too excited for Christmas to sleep.

I woke first, sometime after 11 last night, on the couch in the living room. Cayley was gone, the TV dark. There was a pillow under my head and a blanket covering me, the lights from the Christmas tree casting everything in a twinkly rainbow glow. I must have slept through everyone getting home.

I staggered down the hall to my own room and collapsed onto the bed, falling straight back to sleep.

And now I'm lying here, far too early to be awake on Christmas morning, watching as the world behind the curtains shifts from darkness to grey.

I know I won't sleep again, especially when thoughts of Essie and Annie crawl out from the dark corners of my mind.

I push back the covers and climb out of bed, throwing on a t-shirt and jeans and a light sweatshirt to fend off that tiny bit of chill.

If I can't sleep, I may as well make myself useful.

I'm in the kitchen whisking together a dozen eggs when Essie wanders in.

She's dressed, in soft pants that could potentially be pyjamas, and a lilac sweatshirt. She's working her fingers through her loose hair, gathering it on top of her head into what I know will be a messy tangle most would refer to as a bun. Her face is bare of any makeup, a rare occasion, and her eyes are still a little sleepy.

The whole look is so sweet and soft, such a stark contrast from the version of Essie the world sees, that I stand there for a moment blinking at her.

She ties off her bun and turns to face me, right as I snap out of it.

"Merry Christmas, Estella," I say, trying to sound bright and not like there's a tangle of vines constricting my throat.

"Merry Christmas, Jackson," she says as she slides onto a stool at the bench. She gives me a soft smile. It's a radical difference from how she's behaved around me since the kissing. "I can't believe I got up early and you still beat me."

I chuckle at her tiny pout. "Sorry, Estella, you know I can't let you win."

"I will one day," she says, attempting to glower at me but letting it give way into a smile instead.

I've missed this version of her. The one that talks to me.

She takes a deep breath and sets something on the bench.

It's the little blue box with the purple ribbon. She slides it across the bench towards me. I set down the bowl of eggs I've been half-heartedly mixing since she got downstairs.

I lean my arms on the bench directly across from her and my fingers brush against hers as they land on the box, stopping it sliding any closer to me.

"I can't accept this, Jackson," she whispers, her eyes avoiding mine.

"Why not, Estella?"

She lifts her face and I meet those green eyes for the first time since the day I kissed her. I hold my breath, waiting for whatever damning words she's going to say.

Her eyes drop away from mine and she gives a little shrug. "I don't know what it means," she says.

I blink in surprise. "What do you mean?" The words come out a little harsher than I intend.

She glances up again. "I don't know why you got me a present."

I smile. She looks so confused. Sometimes I forget that she's still seventeen, an age when, at times, everyone's motivations feel questionable.

"There's no ulterior motive," I say, wondering how I'm going to find the right words to effectively say what I need to and not overdo or undermine the reasons and feelings. "I saw it and thought of you immediately. You still hated me then though, so I didn't get it. But later…" I stop and haul in a deep breath. "Estella, sometimes I give presents to people I care about, okay?"

"But … the other day. We agreed that was a mistake. We can't … we can't do that … be that."

I want to tell her I never agreed to any such thing, but it's obvious this is what she wants. I'll let the worry that I overstepped the line come later. For now I need to reassure this girl in front of me, who's still looking sleepy and confused and like she's waiting for the catch.

"I bought a present for Cayley," I say. "Sometimes friends give each other presents. Can I care about you without you thinking there's ulterior motive?"

"We're friends?" She blinks at me, surprise shaping her features.

I look at her, exasperated. Our fingers are both still fiddling with the box in the middle of the bench between us and I feel a little zap every time they connect. "Yes Estella, if you want to be, we're friends. I'm going to consider you my friend regardless." I pause, watching as her fingers still on the box. I carefully place mine tip to tip with hers, the barest touch between us. Then I lift my gaze to meet hers once more. "The other night on the beach … I don't normally talk to people about that stuff." A trembling inhale. "You're my friend, Estella."

She sucks in a breath, sliding her fingers forward so they press against mine. I shift slightly, covering her hands with mine and squeezing softly as I push the box back towards her.

"Accept it, Estella. It won't suit me."

She cracks a smile and takes the box. My hands fall away as she pulls it out of my reach, her fingers slipping from mine. I'm trying not to think about entwining our fingers together and how her palm would feel against mine.

"Can I open it now?"

I nod. "I thought you'd open it when I gave it to you," I say. "I'm impressed you didn't. I would have opened it straight away."

She gasps up at me. "I didn't get you anything." Her lips tug downwards.

I shrug. "It's okay. I don't need anything. Open it."

She pulls at the bow and the ribbon gives way, softly falling to the counter. The box lid sticks for a moment before it comes free and she gazes down into the box. "Oh, Jax." She breathes, then looks up. "Jackson, they're gorgeous."

I smile, a bubble of joy spreading through my chest. "Told you they wouldn't suit me," I say, and turn back to my eggs.

Chapter Thirty-Five

ESSIE

I HELP my friend Jax make breakfast.

Well, I cut up some strawberries because that's as much as he'll let me do, which seems fair considering he's seen my attempts in the kitchen.

The little box with my favourite Christmas present in it sits beside me. I don't even have to see my other presents to know that none of them will top this one.

I get distracted by staring at it and poke myself with the knife. "Ouch." I inspect my finger for damage but it's barely broken the skin.

"You all right?" Jax asks, stepping over the stovetop where he's cooking the largest batch of French toast I've ever seen.

"Yeah, tried to stab myself," I say, a light burn finding my cheeks. Apparently even slicing fruit is too much for my kitchen skills.

"See this bit?" He reaches over the bench and points to the knife blade. "It's very sharp, quite pointy. That's the bit you keep away from your hands."

I throw a strawberry at him. He catches it, grins and bites into it. He's so cocky and smug. He's also … happy.

"You're such an ass," I grumble, but his happiness is contagious. Just knowing that he's happy makes me happy.

"Yet somehow I'm your friend." He grins again, like this little fact has made his day.

"I never actually said you were mine," I say haughtily.

He winks at me, and though I want to throw another strawberry or perhaps even the knife at him, I laugh instead.

"You didn't have to, Estella."

He turns back to the stove, easily flipping the latest batch.

I go back to the strawberries and staring at the present, though I'm a little more cautious with the knife now.

I'm still stunned he got me a present. I'm also stunned I went two days without opening it to discover exactly what was inside.

Setting the knife down, I pick up the box again, running my fingers over the earrings nestled into soft pink tissue paper. They're big hoops, but made up of several strands of silver twining together. The best part is, the strands themselves are made of stars of different sizes. There's nothing uniform about them, only dozens of tiny stars strung together. I've never seen something so gorgeous in my life.

I glance up to see Jax watching me, a little smile on his face. "You like them?"

"I love them," I say. "Where did you find them?"

"At that market," he says. "There's a card in the box. You should look the girl up, she had some cool stuff."

"You got me these that long ago? I didn't even like you then."

He laughs, the sound bright and free, like he loves me

throwing my distaste for him in his face. "I saw them then. I didn't buy them until a few days ago. I was worried they weren't going to turn up in time."

A few days ago. My brain does the maths. "After…" My words trail off but my gaze travels to that spot on the kitchen bench where I sat with him pressing kisses to my skin.

Jax takes three swift steps across the kitchen and stands directly across the bench from me, leaning down to stare me in the eye. "No, Estella. Before that. When we got home the night before that."

After the beach, then. That's all right. I let the breath I've been holding go, gently, so Jax doesn't notice I was holding it.

"Before that day I wasn't sure if you'd have thrown them back in my face or not."

I laugh this time. "Don't know what you're talking about."

We grin at each other, then Jax sneaks another strawberry and goes back to his stove.

I scold him. "There'll be none left if you keep eating them."

"Eating them is the point, Estella."

"You know, the next thing I throw at you won't be another strawberry." I pause. "Or the earrings, because they're far too pretty. And the only other thing I have handy is this knife you described as sharp and pointy."

"You wouldn't dare." He turns back to me, that smug look back on his face. I can't believe I used to hate it.

"Don't test me, Jackson Sherwood."

He raises his hands in surrender, right as Mum walks into the room.

"I really hope you aren't planning to throw that knife at our guest," she says wearily.

“I’m strongly considering it,” I say, “but only because he deserves it.” With my free hand I carefully slide the earrings off the counter and into the box on my lap. I replace the lid before slipping the box into my hoodie pocket. Jax’s eyes follow my movement, a little nod of understanding. There’ll be too many questions if my family know he’s got me a present, especially one this gorgeous, and I can’t be bothered defending it right now.

“He’s cooking breakfast,” Mum says, a rare smile tugging at her lips. “If you must impale him can you at least wait until after he’s finished?”

I pretend to carefully weigh up her words, all the while tapping the knife against the chopping board. “I see your reasoning,” I say eventually.

“Plus, Christmas seems a poor choice of day,” Jax says, flipping another piece of toast. “I wouldn’t want you to have to spend Christmas Day in jail.”

“Who says I’m going to jail?”

“For the murder you’re threatening to commit in my kitchen?” Mum asks. “I think a lot of people would say you’d be going to jail. Most of all me. Think of the mess it’d make.”

I shrug, a smile continually fighting to curve my mouth upwards. “Jax likes a tidy kitchen. I’m sure he’ll clean it up for you.”

“Reminder Estella, I’ll be dead. Remember, knife thrown at my body.”

I laugh now as Mum sits beside me, stealing herself a strawberry. I shoot her a joking scowl. “You guys really overestimate my ability to throw a knife. And stop eating all the strawberries or there won’t be any left.”

Jax sets a huge plate down in front of us, stacked high with French toast. "Ready when you guys are."

Mum turns to me, and before she asks I'm already hopping off my chair.

"I'll go get David," I say, only slightly gleeful that I get to wake him on Christmas. "There'd better be some strawberries left when I get back."

Chapter Thirty-Six

JAX

I SPEND my first Christmas without my own mother.

It's a weird kind of day, waking up on a sofa bed in a room that's not really mine.

But then Essie helped me make breakfast and I felt like I was in exactly the place I was supposed to be.

Occasionally I glanced at her and found her gazing in reverence at the earrings. It was a huge relief, that she accepted the gift and that she loved it.

It's also a huge relief that we've mended whatever happened after the apparently never-to-be-mentioned-again kissing. I've missed her far too much since that day.

But joking with her in the kitchen was the best part of this weird Christmas Day.

I eat breakfast with Essie, David, Miriam and Karl, sitting across the table from Essie, sharing smiles as her family laughs and jokes.

"What's the challenge this year?" Essie asks, after sliding yet another piece of French toast onto her plate and drowning it in maple syrup.

"Golf," Karl says with a wicked grin. His wife and children stare at him in open-mouthed horror.

"Golf?" Essie says. "Like mini golf, yeah?"

Karl shakes his head. "No, like actual golf."

David groans and actually bangs his head against the table. Miriam says nothing but her face looks a little pained too.

I turn to Essie, confusion on my face. She glances at me, swallows her mouthful and explains. "Every year we take turns deciding on the Christmas activity. It's supposed to be something we don't do regularly and it's a bonus if there's some kind of competition involved."

I blink at her. My Christmases involve presents that are mostly average, food, which is generally pretty good, and seeing relatives who most of the time I don't want to see. They ask inane questions about my life and make judgements on the meagre facts those questions garner.

"Last year Essie made us go to the beach and build sandcastles as tall as we were," David says with an eye roll, but it must be the mocking sort because there's a touch of a smile on his face. "It was convenient for her because she's the shortest."

Essie laughs and shrugs. "I've gotta find my advantage somehow."

"And none of you normally play golf?" I ask.

Essie shakes her head. "Dad has done before on the rare occasion, but the rest of us, nope. It's going to be a disaster."

"Epic disaster," David agrees.

I don't think I've ever heard them agree on something, so it takes me a little while to speak. "I'm really, really sorry I'm going to miss it," I say.

"You're not coming?" Essie's eyes flash to mine then flick towards her parents.

"I'm going to see Aunt Kate," I say hurriedly before she gets the chance to accuse her parents of kicking me out for the day. "She's insisted I be there. I would normally spend a whole lot of Christmas with them anyway. But I am quite disappointed I don't get to watch you two play golf." I glance towards David as well, to include him, so it's not all about Essie, though most of the time I forget I'm staying here because of him and not her.

Essie steals the last strawberry off the serving plate, waving it triumphantly at me. We finish the meal with the family settling back into laughing, joking and gentle ribbing. Predictions are made for golf placings. I can see Essie's competitiveness sparking up.

It's an interesting dynamic. For so long Essie has been at odds with her parents, mostly over the way she's spending her time these holidays. I don't know if it was ever discussed further. Essie hasn't mentioned anything to me since the night of their big fight and our trip to the beach. But then, we haven't been talking much since then. If I were to calculate it, I'd say we've done more kissing than talking since that night.

But today that animosity has been set aside. I noticed it the moment Miriam stepped into the kitchen while Essie was threatening to throw knives at me.

I never really fought with Mum. I don't know if it was that I never pushed the boundaries, she never really set boundaries for me to push, or we simply met in the middle and it wasn't ever an issue. I wonder if it had anything to do with it being me and her against the world, barely making it through some days.

But I miss her now. I miss sitting in our little house with her drinking three cups of coffee on Christmas morning while we exchange one meaningful gift each, then moving on to Aunt Kate's for the far more extravagant family affair.

Even surrounded by people it's hard not to feel a little bit alone.

"Right, David, you're on clean up," Miriam says, pushing her chair back and standing from the table.

"Wait, what? How come Essie doesn't have to help?"

"Because Essie helped make breakfast," Miriam says, and I notice the smile tugging at Essie's lips. I wish she wouldn't try to suppress it. I like seeing her happy and free.

"Come on, man," I say, getting up and stacking plates together, giving him a shove with my elbow as I do. "I'll help."

Essie stands and picks up the stack of plates. "And me," she says with a dramatic sigh. "Wouldn't want you to overdo it this morning, David."

He scowls at her as she waltzes towards the kitchen. He glances at me. "What's with her this morning?"

I blink at him. Give an awkward shrug. "What … what do you mean?"

"She's, I dunno, pleasant," he says, his gaze following her.

I shrug again. "Oh, she's not that bad," I say, picking up another pile of plates.

His eyes flash back to mine and I meet his gaze, knowing avoiding it will make me look suspicious. "What's she done to you?"

"What?" I croak, hoping the heat I can feel sneaking across my skin isn't obvious to him.

"She's corrupted your brain. Didn't you hate her?"

I glance towards Essie, who's stacking the dishwasher, humming Christmas carols badly. "No. I've never hated her. She's actually pretty cool, man. Don't be so hard on her. And she's doing your job right now so you should be a little more grateful."

He sits for another moment, then stands. "Yeah, suppose she's all right … sometimes." He picks up the maple syrup and the empty strawberry bowl. "Oh, and hey, Merry Christmas, dude."

He gives me a little shunt as he walks past and I know that's the most affection I'll ever receive from this guy.

"You too, David."

Chapter Thirty-Seven

ESSIE

CHRISTMAS IS A WEIRD DAY.

There's really no other way to describe it.

First there's the moments spent with Jax making breakfast and opening the most gorgeous gift to ever exist. Laughing with him in the kitchen feels so natural, like it's exactly the right place for me to be, watching him as he flips french toast in the frying pan, whisks eggs and beats cream with his sleeves pushed up to the elbows so I can trail my gaze over the firm muscles of his forearms.

He grins at me each time he glances in my direction, which is often. I smile back and mentally scold myself for pulling away this week, for missing all those days when I could have been with my friend.

Mum is clearly in a good mood, joking with us in the kitchen like it happens all the time. We don't fight, don't even disagree about anything.

Even David is less of a jerk than usual, and golf might actually be … fun? If my family can hold together this unusual mood. It'd definitely be fun if Jax was coming with us.

I wish he could, but when I come down the stairs after getting dressed he's at the front door, shoving his feet into sneakers. It's a shock seeing him in good clothes – a button-down shirt and pants that aren't jeans – rather than his work ones or a simple t-shirt.

He glances up at me, but before I have the chance to speak to him, Mum interrupts.

"Oh, Essie, those are lovely earrings," she says, pausing on her way from kitchen to living room with coffee for her and Dad to help them get through present opening.

"Oh," I say, reaching up to brush my fingertips across them. "Thanks. They're from a friend."

Her eyes narrow slightly, but she carries on into the next room after saying goodbye to Jax and confirming we'll see him for dinner. My gaze lands on him, leaning against the front door. He has a little smile curling at his mouth, like hearing me refer to him as a friend has made his day.

He pushes off the door and steps closer. "They really are lovely," he says with a smirk. "You have excellent friends."

I smile, and his spreads wider in response. "If they were truly excellent they'd be sticking around, not abandoning me to golf with my family."

He chuckles. "You'll be fine. You never know, it might even be fun."

We've drifted closer together, meeting in the middle of the entry foyer without me even realising how I've got here, and now I can feel the heat off his body, sense every little shift he makes.

He clears his throat. "I should get going." His voice is a little rough and he doesn't look at all like he wants to leave.

I nod. "I'll see you later."

Neither of us moves.

My breath hitches at his closeness, the way he's staring at me.

He blinks like he's startled and shifts away. It breaks me from the spell I'm under, the one he casts whenever he gets too close, and I immediately miss him being so near.

"Right, going now," he says, clearing his throat. "See you later," he mutters as he reaches for the door.

My hand reaches out, tangling my fingers with his, stopping him leaving. "I never said thank you," I say.

He turns back to me and his eyes flick between our hands, extended between us, and my face.

"So, thank you Jackson, for my present."

A blast of extremely loud music, some Christmas carol, comes from the living room and I jump in fright, my hand slipping from Jax's. I glare towards my family, out of sight in the next room, and when I turn back to Jax he's gone, the door closing quietly behind him.

As it turns out, Jax is correct and golf is actually fun. Mostly because we are all entirely terrible at it, even Dad, and being Christmas, everyone seems in a fairly good mood.

There's no arguing, no barbed comments, no overly heavy sighs aimed in my direction.

Instead, we laugh until we cry when David repeatedly misses his final tee shot, while he scolds us for making him laugh so he has no chance of making a good shot.

Once David finally makes his shot and Mum and I take our turn at the tee, Dad steps up, flexing like he's got this in the bag. But he's even worse than the rest of us and we dissolve into fits of giggles again.

It's taken hours for us to play nine holes, and even when the competitiveness comes out near the end it's good natured and sprinkled with snatches of badly sung Christmas songs and laughter.

It reminds me that I do actually like my family a lot of the time. The times when they aren't pressuring me into some obscene career that involves spending years at university learning science-y things I'll never comprehend, and working all hours in an office or emergency vet clinic, even on Christmas Eve.

Both my parents worked late last night, dealing with some emergency animal surgery, then had dinner together on their way home.

It suited me fine because David was working too, and Jeremy invited me to hang out with him.

At the time I didn't even think about Jax being at home alone on Christmas Eve – until I found him asleep with Cayley on the couch.

I didn't want to think about Jax being upset with me, or hurt by me. I didn't want to care about him. It wasn't until my conversation with Cayley, quietly sipping pink tea in my kitchen on Christmas Eve, that I realised I do care. I care about Jax and I care that I might have hurt him by trying to protect myself from getting hurt by him.

I'm glad he had Cayley last night. After she left I draped him with a blanket, tucking the fluffy grey fabric gently around his shoulders, and stuck a note on the front door telling the rest of my family that Jax was sleeping in the lounge and to be quiet.

I wonder briefly what he's doing now as I watch Mum lining up the putt that should see her win. I should know better, because as I've realised, someone in my family can mess up even the simplest of shots.

She misses and we howl with laughter. Dad has to sit down, tears of laughter running down his cheeks.

In that moment, I forget all about the expectations and judgements, and simply love my family.

Chapter Thirty-Eight

JAX

WHEN I GET HOME on New Year's Eve Essie is back in the kitchen.

I've been at work. I don't have anything better to do except avoid calls from Annie, who still thinks I'm going to take her back, so I offered to go in and help out today. It's weirdly quiet with most of the guys off on holiday, but there's still plenty of urgent work to be done.

The kitchen is surprisingly orderly considering Essie is in it, with ingredients lined up along one bench, measuring cups and spoons sitting alongside mixing bowls and baking trays.

Essie is leaning against the bench, chewing her lip and poring over a recipe book.

"Should I ask?" I say, sliding onto the stool across from where she's standing.

She glances up at me and her whole face lights up. I blink at her. She doesn't hate me anymore but I'm not usually the recipient of such smiles.

Things have been good since Christmas. The mood between Essie and her parents, even between Essie and David, seems to have lightened. Maybe they all needed to have a bit of fun together and remember they might like each other, deep down.

My friendship with Essie has settled too. We're back to where we were before the kissing. She hangs out with me when I'm home, sewing while I study or cook.

"Brooke's coming home today," Essie tells me, grin stretching even wider.

My mind goes blank. How do I not know who Brooke is? "Brooke …" I say, trying to kickstart my brain.

Essie rolls her eyes. "My best friend," she says.

Oh. How do I not even know who her best friend is?

"Where's she been?"

"Visiting her dad since the day school finished."

Right, because other people's dads still want to have something to do with them. I'm not usually affected too much by thoughts of my father. I guess it's hard to miss something you never had. But occasionally I'm struck by this wistfulness or something, which makes me miss the life I could have had if he'd been a better person.

I'm the age he was when he found out Mum was pregnant, and though it's definitely not my plan to end up a teenage parent, if it happened I wouldn't do a runner.

I'd be terrified, but I wouldn't run.

I refocus on Essie. Nothing good lies in that train of thought. "And you're trying to scare her away again with your baking?"

She narrows her eyes into a steely glare, but I can see her fighting her smile. "It's why I'm so pleased to see you, dear Jackson. I wanted to make her something."

"Ah, you want my help again." I pause, tapping my fingers

on the benchtop like I'm thinking about it. "All right, but this time you'll be doing it and I'll teach you some things." I slide off the stool. When I glance up at Essie her cheeks have turned pink. She gives me a quick nod and spins around, taking her recipe book to the other side of the kitchen. I think about what I've said, and I think about what happened last time Essie was baking.

I clear my throat, ridding it of a sudden blockage as I remember the feel of Essie's skin against my palms and my lips. There's heat spreading across my face now and I'm so relieved she isn't looking at me. "Uh, give me a few minutes to clean up, okay?"

She nods, barely glancing my way. "Yup."

Another super-speedy shower and I'm back in the kitchen. Essie's face has returned to its normal colour. I'm hoping mine has done the same.

"What're we making?" I ask as I stand beside Essie at the counter. She's got three books spread out before her, all open to a different version of the same recipe. "Chocolate chip cookies, by the looks of it," I say before she has a chance to answer.

"Yes," she says with a heavy sigh. "But I can't figure out which one is the easiest or best to make."

I flip the books closed and stack them neatly on the end of the bench. "None of them," I say, and pull out my phone. "There's only one recipe for chocolate chip cookies, and it's Aunt Kate's. I'll write it out for you, but start with your butter. Have you softened it?"

She stares at me. Her lips, painted bright pink again, are

parted in confusion as she slowly blinks. "How about you pretend like I know absolutely nothing about baking and teach me every step?"

"Estella, you do know absolutely nothing about baking. There'll be no pretending."

She punches my shoulder, but she's laughing. "Shut up, Jackson. Show me what to do."

We move through the steps and it's weirdly sentimental sharing this recipe with someone else. I know the process by heart from making it at least once a week throughout my childhood, often with Cayley and Melissa, even though they were only there to lick the bowl when I was done. These chocolate chip cookies were the first present I ever gave my mum, when I was old enough to realise that there was no one else to give her presents except Aunt Kate. So I baked a huge batch and put them in a box with a bow on the top, giving them to her for Mother's Day. She cried. I gave her another batch every year.

As we work, when Essie isn't silent while concentrating, she talks about Brooke, saying that if I'm her friend like I claim to be, then I should know who her best friend is.

"So she got home this morning, and we're supposed to be going to this party tonight but Dad has this stupid rule that I'm not allowed to drive on New Year's."

"Really?"

She catches my confused expression and elaborates. "He says it's not about me or that he doesn't trust me, it's that he doesn't trust other people on the road. Which doesn't make a lot of sense because I'm allowed to be in a car on New Year's Eve, I'm just not allowed to be driving a car on New Year's Eve." She pauses, then says, "Well, I'm allowed to be in a car if my parents approve the driver."

"Huh. I kind of get it in some ways," I say, and immediately hold my hands up in an "I surrender" gesture before she has a chance to fire up at me. "People are idiots at the best of times, Estella. They're only trying to reduce the risk."

She sighs. "I know, but it still doesn't help me get to this party tonight."

"It depends," I say, thinking aloud. "Would I make the approved drivers list?"

She turns to me, eyes wide with excitement. "Yes," she breathes. "Are you sure?"

"Of course. I suspect I'm going to the same party."

"And we can pick up Brooke?"

"Of course."

She throws herself at me, wrapping her arms around my waist, squeezing me tight. "Thank you, thank you, thank you," she says into my t-shirt.

I laugh and wrap my arms around her back, holding her close. She somehow smells like butter and vanilla.

She hugs me for a long moment, but when she pulls away it's still too soon. I'm beginning to suspect it will always be too soon. I'll always want more.

"I'll text Brooke now. Thank you so much."

I smile at her. "Don't let your cookies burn."

She gasps and I let out a laugh. I can't contain the happiness in me.

"I'll get the cookies out then I'll text Brooke," she says.

"You'd better check with your dad, too," I say, suddenly worried I've got her hopes up way too high.

She waves my comment away. "That won't be a problem. He thinks you're wonderful." She pauses, our eyes meet and she gives a little shrug. "And maybe he's not the only one."

Chapter Thirty-Nine

ESSIE

I CLIMB into the front seat of Jax's car and settle the plastic container of cookies on my lap. With his help they turned out near perfect and utterly delicious. They're still slightly warm and the smell fills the interior of the car.

Until Jax slides into the driver's seat and wipes it away with his clean masculine scent. It's undercut with lingering traces of butter and sugar and I want to lean into him and inhale.

I bounce slightly in my seat instead, shifting my thoughts away from Jax and back to Brooke. I can't believe she's finally home.

Jax grins over at me but doesn't say anything as he reverses out of the driveway.

We spend the short trip to Brooke's in silence, aside from me giving him directions and one of us occasionally humming along to the radio, but unlike the early days, it's not awkward or uncomfortable or even antagonistic. It's content, comfortable, pleasant. Even as he sneaks little looks over at me while I grin out the windscreen and occasionally give the container of cookies a little shake, satisfied with the sound they make inside.

I don't think I've ever been prouder of anything.

"It's this one here," I say, and Jax smoothly pulls into the driveway.

Brooke is sitting on her front porch swing but leaps up when she sees us. I jump out of the car and run to meet her, wrapping my arms around her. I bump her in the back of the head with the cookie container.

She squeals and holds me at arm's length, eyes travelling up and down me. "I've missed you so much," she says, pulling me in for another hug.

"Saaaame," I say, leaning into her.

"Essie," she says, muttering into my hair as she holds me tight. "Is our ride Jax Sherwood?"

I pull out of her hug and grin at her. "Yes, it is," I say, glancing over my shoulder to see Jax leaning on the driver's side door of his car, smiling indulgently at me. "You can also thank him that your welcome home present is edible." I hand her the box and she lifts the corner of the lid to peek inside.

"Oooh." Her eyes light up. "I didn't know you could bake anything."

"I couldn't," I mutter, and she laughs. "Hence why you should thank Jax. He's really good." My eyes meet his as we start towards the car and I feel a little flicker of something in my chest.

It's a feeling I've been experiencing fairly regularly of late. I'm still refusing to acknowledge it means I have a crush.

On Jax.

Of all people.

I'm constantly catching myself thinking about the day we sat on the beach, and the day after – in the kitchen. I almost sewed right over my finger earlier today because I was daydreaming about the feeling of Jax's hands on my waist.

He slides back into his seat as Brooke and I approach the car and get in ourselves.

"Hi, Brooke," Jax says, flashing her one of his grins over his shoulder as he reverses out of the driveway.

"Jax." She gives him a solemn nod. Before I have a chance to say anything, she continues. "What've you done to Essie?"

I twist to face her in the backseat. "What? Brooke!"

The corner of Jax's mouth tugs upwards. "I don't know what you mean," he says.

"Well …" Brooke settles back into her seat and from the look on her face I know she's going to come out with something ridiculous and likely mortifying. "She hated you three weeks ago."

"Brooke!" I cry again.

"So, I'm wondering," Brooke continues as if I haven't said anything, "what it was you did to her to bend her to your will. Is it something I could use against her?"

Jax laughs out loud and I shoot him a glare. "Hated me, huh?" he says, the laugh still sparkling in his eyes.

"Yeah, well, you were a jerk to me," I mutter, slumping into my seat and glaring at Brooke's reflection in the wing mirror.

"I hung around a lot and cooked her food," Jax says to Brooke. "Do you still hate me?" he says to me, gaze flicking between the road and me. His mouth has gone tight, the corners turning down slightly.

I squirm under his gaze. "No," I say.

My hand lands on his arm. It's outstretched, his hand resting on the gear stick. He's wearing a mint-green dress shirt with his jeans tonight. The sleeves are rolled up, like always, and my hand flares with heat as it connects with his bare skin. I squeeze softly. "We're friends, remember?"

He shoots me a little smile, eyes flickering to the earrings I'm wearing, the starry hoops he gave me for Christmas. His hand twists and he grasps my fingers for barely a second before he releases. "Of course."

We pull into the party. It's a couple of kids from school throwing it. Twins in David and Jax's year, and their younger brother. I'm surprised their parents let them have a massive party for New Year. It's hard enough getting my parents to let me have half a dozen girls in our house to celebrate my birthday. I tend to have my birthday parties elsewhere now.

But as we pull in, Jax drives past the house, a giant sprawling thing with perfectly manicured gardens, and heads for a big shed further back. He parks in the paddock and we all climb out, Brooke with a cookie in her mouth.

"These are really bloody good," she says, leaning her head against my shoulder with her arm around my waist. It feels so good to have her back. She's a super touchy person, very affectionate, giving love wherever she goes, and it's soothing to be bathed in her glow once again.

Jax locks the car, sliding the key into his pocket. "Anytime you guys want to go let me know, okay?"

"Sure, Jackson," I say, falling into step beside him and linking my arm through his as we make our way across the grass. I'm glad I chose flat shoes for tonight. He pats my hand where it rests against his forearm, letting his fingers linger over mine. I'm enjoying the new level of friendship we've achieved, in which touching is acceptable. Or maybe it's that Jax has got over his weird "will not touch Essie" thing. Either way, I like it.

"I'm serious." He leans down to whisper in my ear and his

breath leaves trails of goosebumps spiralling across my skin. "Anytime either of you want to go. Otherwise we're out of here by 1 am."

"Yes, Jackson," I say. "I know." Then I drop the sarcasm, the exasperation, from my voice. "Thank you. I really do appreciate this."

We've stopped at the edge of the party. Groups of teenagers are standing around out the front of the large shed. A few old couches are scattered about, some deck chairs and hay bales. There's a brazier burning in the middle of it all, lighting everything in a bright orange glow. Music thrums through the night. The stars burn bright above.

Jax moves forward, stepping into the halo of light, but Brooke tugs me back before I can follow him.

He turns back as my hand slips from his arm, a questioning look on his face. "You coming?"

"We'll catch up with you soon," I say.

He smiles. It's not his usual grin. It's that soft one that gently curves his lip and crinkles the corners of his eyes ever so slightly. It hits me straight in the heart.

As he walks away Brooke rests her chin on my shoulder, watching him go. "You never told me it was like this," she says thoughtfully.

"Like what?" I ask, still watching Jax as he greets a couple of people.

"I don't know how to say it." She pauses, leaning into me. "When you said he wasn't so bad, and that you were sort of friends, I thought you meant like, casual, in-passing sort of friends. Like, a little more than acquaintances, and mostly it was only to keep the peace while you were living together. But it's not like that."

"What's it like, then?" I ask, confusion clouding my voice. I'm not sure I want to hear her take on this. I value her opinion too much and I'm not sure I can handle her telling me the truth.

"Close friends. Or even more than that. I think he actually likes you."

I snort. "You think he *actually* likes me? Why do you sound so surprised? But yes, we're friends; liking the other person is sort of a prerequisite." Inside, I'm startled. Brooke is notoriously good at reading people. It's kind of terrifying, her intuition about these things. I know exactly what she means when she says he "likes" me. I'm still refusing to let myself acknowledge it, though.

We had that one stupid moment and he's never made a move again. We agreed to never talk about it. We've moved on from that kiss.

Except I haven't actually moved on, because I think about that kiss at least five times a day. Minimum.

Brooke squeezes me tight. "Don't be silly, Essie. You know what I mean. The way he watches you, there's definitely something there. And that's not to mention the way you look at him."

I turn to face her. "Why am I happy you're home, again?"

She laughs and hugs me tight. Leading me into the party, she says, "You know I'm right, Es. Don't kill it before it even begins."

Chapter Forty

JAX

ESSIE TOUCHES ME SO CASUALLY, over and over.

I wonder if she would have been touching me like this the whole time we've been hanging out if I hadn't been so adamantly against touching *her*.

The places she's touched tonight are still warm and tingly. My forearm where she lightly squeezed my arm in the car, my fingertips where I recklessly gripped hers in mine, the inside of my wrist where her fingers brushed as she walked with her arm through mine, her body so close I could feel the heat of her, even through jeans.

I left Brooke and Essie to it once we arrived at the party. Brooke obviously needed time to catch up with Essie alone, and as much as I want to spend every single second in Essie's presence, I know she needs her other friends too.

I grab a can of Coke from the drinks table and head towards where I can see Cayley and a few of our friends sprawled across a couch. I lean against the end of it, ruffling Cayley's hair in greeting.

"Who're those girls you were with?" A voice pipes up from the far end of the couch. Zoe. One of Annie's best friends. Fabulous.

Everyone turns to me awaiting my answer, and I'm immediately on the defensive. I don't need to explain myself to any of them, but aside from Zoe, no one is looking at me like they want scandalous gossip.

"Essie and Brooke," I say with a shrug.

"Oh, you brought Essie?" Cayley says, turning to me with a smile. I see Zoe's face pinch as I turn away, facing my cousin.

"Yep," I say.

"Oh, yay. She's so much fun," Cayley says, and though she can't see Zoe's face, the look on Cayley's lets me know she knows exactly the reaction the other girl is having.

My friends return to their previous conversations and I settle more comfortably on the arm of the couch next to Cayley, asking for an update on the wedding plans.

Aunt Kate asked me on Christmas Day to be a part of the ceremony, to walk her down the aisle. I tried to deny her, saying Cayley and Melissa should be the ones to do it, but Kate insisted, ensuring me the girls were more than happy for me to do it.

Cayley fires a million updates at me, including when she's booked a suit fitting for me, and I make a note in my phone so I don't forget.

She's mid-sentence about the hair trial, whatever that is, when her attention is caught by something behind me. "Essie!" she calls, waving frantically.

I glance over my shoulder and realise Essie is right there behind me. I've been trying to spot her in the crowd since I sat down, but she was behind my line of sight, hanging in the near-shadow at the edge of the firelight's reach.

I watch as she walks towards us, a little hesitantly, Brooke beside her nudging her along.

"Hi." I reach out and gently grasp her upper arm, right above her elbow. The touch feels so natural, but that fire flares through my blood again and I drop my hand back to my lap, pressing my burning fingers against my cool Coke can.

Cayley starts chattering away a million miles an hour and I notice Zoe stalking off into the night as Essie excitedly updates Cayley on the status of the dresses.

"Oh, these are those dresses you showed me the pictures of?" Brooke asks Essie, her eyes alight. Essie nods and Brooke turns to Cayley. "Oh my gosh, they're so gorgeous."

Cayley beams. "I know. Essie's so clever."

Essie beams too.

Cayley suddenly hauls herself up from the couch, using me as a grab rail. "You're coming to dance with us, right?" she asks Essie as she slides her hand behind my elbow, giving me a tug firm enough to unseat me.

Essie hesitates.

"Who do you mean by 'us', Cayley?" I say, trying to sit back down though her grip is still far too tight to let me.

"You and me. Essie and Brooke are coming. Aren't you?"

She turns back to the girls. Brooke is grinning wickedly. I can see why Essie loves her so much, but I really don't appreciate them all ganging up on me.

"Of course," Brooke chirps, grabbing Essie by the arm.

"Uh, I wasn't …" Essie starts, and I've cut her off before I realise I've done it.

"Cayley, you know I'm not going to dance. I never dance."

"Jackson Sherwood," she says, voice stern. "It is New Year's Eve and you are going to come and dance with your cousin, who is also your best friend ever, and our other friends, okay?"

Essie snorts, but it doesn't feel mean when I notice she's slipping her arm through mine again. "Yeah, come on Jackson Sherwood, it's New Year's Eve."

"You'll keep, Estella Markham," I mutter to her, and something in me takes flight when she laughs and tips her head to rest against my shoulder for a moment before she and Cayley tug me forwards.

Her hand is so warm and so soft against the inside of my wrist. I wonder if she can feel the way my pulse is racing.

"No one's even dancing," I hiss at Cayley.

She shrugs. "Someone has to be the first, Jax."

Then she begins to move to the music. She takes Essie's hand, pulling her into the dance, spinning her around.

The skirt of Essie's dress flares as she twirls, white sneakers flashing against the grass. Brooke dances beside them, all three girls shaking their hair back, tipping their faces to the sky and raising their hands in the air.

I stand in the shadow, out of the reach of the light, feeling the music vibrate out of the speaker I'm hiding behind.

A few other girls congregate and soon there's a whole bunch of people dancing. Cayley was right, they only needed one person to start it. And of course it was Cayley and Essie.

I watch them.

Well, I watch Essie.

She looks incredible tonight in her midnight blue dress with the fitted top and swirling skirt, wide straps tied in bows on top of her shoulders. Her hair is mostly out, curling down her back, but the top section is pulled up high.

She's wearing my earrings. The earrings I gave her. They catch the light, twinkling like real stars as she moves.

She stops dancing, her eyes landing on me even as I'm hiding over here in the shadows. In a moment she's in front of me. Green eyes gaze up at me, framed in silver and blue eye makeup, her lashes dark and long with flicks of black eyeliner enhancing the shape. Her lips are that bright, bold pink again. It's the colour I always think of when I think of her. Even fifty years from now, when I think of Essie, I'll think of that colour.

"Dance with me?" she says, her voice soft and breathy, but somehow I can hear it over the noise of the party.

I open my mouth, ready to say no, because I never dance. It's not something I do, ever.

She takes a sharp breath and her fingers slide into mine. I catch my breath and the words die in my throat as our palms press together, fingers tangling.

"Please?"

I set my drink on the ground, tucking it in beside the speaker so it doesn't get knocked over. Then I step out into the light, Essie's free hand curled around my bicep as she leads me forward, where, with her, I dance.

ESSIE

JAX IS DANCING. Even Cayley seems surprised.

When she pulled us up and encouraged us to dance with her, I wasn't expecting Jax to slip back into the shadows.

"Where'd Jax go?" I shouted into Cayley's ear, trying to be heard over the music.

She shook her head. "Hiding over there. He was right, he doesn't ever dance." Her eyes sparked then, and I'm not sure if they simply caught the light or if it was to do with the words she said next. "Maybe he would with you, though."

She whirled away before I had a chance to reply. Not that I had any words left to say. I continued to dance, letting the music sweep over me. I'll never understand people who say they don't like music. I can understand not liking a certain type of music. But to not like it at all … it will never make sense. It's the soundtrack to every day of my life. I'll never forget that Casey Barnes was playing in the kitchen that day Jax kissed me.

The small detail of me listening to a lot of Casey Barnes over the past two weeks has nothing at all to do with anything.

My eyes kept landing on Jax as he stood in the shadows. I couldn't be sure, but it felt like he was watching me.

That, along with Cayley's and Brooke's comments, had me walking towards him, asking him, sliding my hand into his, intertwining our fingers.

Our hands are still linked now. I expected he'd let go of me once we got close to the others, but he didn't. He moved awkwardly at first, stiff and self-conscious. It's especially endearing considering Jax is always so self-assured.

But as he twirls me around, moving with me as I dance, never letting go of my hand, he loosens up. He's exceptional at spinning me and I laugh wildly as he does, tipping my head back and catching sight of the stars above.

As we dance his free hand brushes against me now and then. A stroke on the shoulder, a touch to my hip, one glorious moment where his fingers linger against my cheek, catching a stray lock of hair and pushing it back behind my shoulder.

Every touch affects me all over again. Rather than getting used to the touches, becoming numb to them, the opposite is happening and each one burns more, sending shivers through me that hit harder every time.

I'm never on edge when Jax touches me. I don't have to worry about where he's going to put his hands. If anything, I want him to touch me more than he does. I want him to touch me in a different way than he does.

I want more.

I step in close to him now, finally sliding my hand free from his. I rest both hands on his shoulders and his eyes flash down to lock with mine, startled.

There's a breath or two before his hands land on my waist. They're big and strong and warm.

I love Jax's hands. It's super weird how often I think about them, complete with small cuts he must get at work, callouses and lingering traces of grease, no matter how often he washes them.

Watching his hands cooking or resting on the steering wheel as he drives is captivating. But there's nothing quite like this feeling of his palms against my waist.

"Smile, Jackson." I lean in to speak into his ear. He exhales sharply, breath hot along my temple. "It's not so bad, is it?"

I slide my hand into his hair at the base of his neck where the soft brown strands start to curl. With my other hand I trail my fingers up his neck, down the length of his jaw, up and across his cheek.

I pull back to study his face, my hand still caressing. His eyes are closed tightly and he looks a long way from smiling. His hands press into my waist, his grip now stiff.

I falter. I thought he was enjoying himself. I thought he wanted to dance with me but was only a bit awkward about it all.

I was wrong.

His eyes slowly open, gazing softly down at me. "Essie." His voice comes out in a low croak, like he has to force the words out. "There's so much … I need … God, Essie, we need to talk abo—"

"You know what?" I cut him off. "I think I need a break and a drink. I'll see you later." I spin away from him. For a second I think he tightens his grip on my waist, trying to pull me back, but that can only be wishful thinking, so I tear myself free of his grasp and disappear into the crowd.

I grab myself a can of Sprite from the drinks table and sulk back into the shadows to lick my wounds, kicking myself for getting so caught up that I actually thought something might be happening between me and Jax.

Of course it wasn't.

I should have known better.

Friends. That's all we are and I'm lucky I get that much of him.

I lean against the corner of the shed, lurking in the dark. I press my back into the cool wall, trying to slow my racing heart. Flashes of memory are circling through my mind in a never-ending parade of moments with Jax. Every one sets my heart racing again.

From sniping at him through to the night we sat on the beach, tears on both our faces, to the kiss in the kitchen, his warm hands finally landing on me.

And then tonight. Dancing under the stars with him, his hand in mine. Or the way my hands slid around his neck, slipping into his hair as I leaned in to speak to him over the noise.

I try to cut the thoughts off there, in that moment when we held each other and everything was perfect.

But my brain won't let me. It replays the seconds right after that, too. On repeat. The tense look on his face, the way his mouth turned down at the corners, his eyes squeezed shut. How he was trying to let me down gently but didn't know how.

I exhale, tipping my head back to stare at the stars.

He'll be gone soon anyway, and I'll have to move on with my life. Might as well start now.

A couple of voices get louder as two girls approach the drinks table, interrupting me trying to make a New Year's resolution to forget all about having any kind of romantic entanglement with Jackson Sherwood. I can't see the girls talking from where I'm hiding in the dark, but one sounds vaguely familiar.

"You're getting back together with Jax?" the voice I don't recognise says.

"Of course," the other says.

I peek around the corner. They're standing right there, pouring something from a bottle into cups.

"What about that girl he came here with?" the dark-haired girl says with a sneer, and I try not to flinch. She doesn't know me at all; her opinion shouldn't matter.

The blonde scoffs. "Essie. She's David's little sister. I don't have anything to worry about there." She turns slightly to place the bottle back on the table and I recognise her.

Annie.

Jax is getting back together with Annie?

I shouldn't be surprised, since he disappeared with her for ages when she arrived at home that day. Right after he'd been kissing me. Maybe that's what he was trying to tell me while we were dancing; that we need to talk because he has to tell me he's giving it another go with her.

"I dunno," the brunette counters. "Did you see them dancing?"

"Yeah, I did. Still not worried." She takes a long pull of her drink. "Did you look at her? She's totally not his type. I heard she's over-dramatic, prone to tantrums and generally a bit *much*. Jax isn't into all that drama. He's being nice to her because he has to. He's living at her place, and he's sweet like that."

Her words are invisible punches straight to the gut. Blow after blow.

The stars blur as tears well.

The brunette girl laughs. “He’s probably just trying to make you jealous or something.” She raises her cup to Annie in a toast. “Let’s go get your man.” Annie taps her cup against her friend’s, then the girls link arms and sashay away, tossing their hair. I couldn’t be that cool and glamorous if I tried.

And I have tried. But I can’t do it. I can’t simply blend in. I wish I could. But Annie is right.

I’ve always been a lot.

Too much.

Always so much drama.

Everyone knows it.

The look Mum gave me as I came downstairs on Christmas, dressed in a bright red dress to play golf, sums it up. I was wearing sneakers and shorts under the dress so it was still practical, but her reaction (and her reaction to most of my outfits) clearly asked why I couldn’t dress normally for once. Maybe a shade or two of black; something without a ruffle or bow or puff sleeve.

David’s said it often enough. I’ve heard him talking to his friends. “Oh, that’s my sister … she’s a *lot*. Just ignore her.”

Even guys have said it to me in the past. I’m fun to be around, but for a girlfriend they want someone soft, someone who stands out in the crowd for being classically gorgeous, not because she insists on wearing green and pink together. They want someone who’ll gently go along with them.

They don’t want someone who’ll threaten to knife them for stealing strawberries, even if it is a joke.

Realisation settles over me, confirming everything I’ve been thinking since I fled from Jax.

This is why he didn’t want to dance with me – because Annie might see and react badly.

I sigh and crumple my now-empty can under my foot. Stamping on it feels good.

Regardless of what Jax is doing, I'm not going to let it ruin my New Year's Eve.

I toss the can, grab another drink and set off to find Brooke, firmly settling that resolution into my heart as I go.

Chapter Forty-Two

JAX

ESSIE WAS HERE, her body against mine, her hand in the hair at the back of my neck, her fingers trailing across my skin.

And now she's gone.

She was here, leaning into me, my hands on the perfect curve of her waist, her breath hot against my ear as she told me to smile.

And before I had a chance to respond, to form the right words after having her so close, having her fill my senses, she was gone, and I'm standing alone amongst a crowd of people dancing, celebrating and making out.

I wanted to kiss her. I wanted to wrap myself around her and never let her go. But there's too much at stake for me to throw myself at her. We need to talk first. We both need to go into this aware of what the fallout is going to look like, and be willing to handle it. Because the fallout will be real, especially where her family – where David – is concerned.

Cayley catches sight of me and shoots me a questioning look, asking about Essie. I shrug and step away from the revellers. Dancing with Essie is one thing; dancing alone is something else entirely, and something I will not be doing.

I return to the couch from earlier, hoping Essie will come back and find me there.

I've barely sat down when someone lands beside me, giggling.

"Hey, Jaxy," Annie says, blinking up at me with big blue eyes. I sigh.

Zoe squeezes in beside Annie, pushing her closer to me, and Annie uses the excuse to fall sideways onto me and leave her hand resting on my thigh.

"How are you?" Annie asks, snuggling even closer.

I shift, trying to put distance between us. "Yeah, fine," I say, my voice hard, sharp, even.

"Who's that with Jeremy?" Zoe interrupts, and at his name my gaze flicks up. "Isn't that the girl you came with, Jax?"

She's right.

Everything in me freezes. My heart is a shard of ice now. My fingers clench on my knees as I stare across the firelight to where Essie is with Jeremy, perched on a hay bale. He reaches out, curling a lock of her hair around his finger. She leans closer.

I'm hit by such a burst of jealousy that it makes me physically jolt.

I tried to do the right thing before kissing her again and potentially ruining everything. My hesitation has ruined it for me anyway.

I wanted so badly to kiss her, or tell her how I feel, and I didn't. I missed my chance.

Maybe I misread the entire situation. She's really physically affectionate with Brooke. Maybe she is with all her friends, and it didn't mean what I thought it meant.

Maybe she figured that out and saved us both the mortification of my stupidity by doing a runner.

I remember her words in the car. "We're friends, remember?"

It would pay for me to remember that. To remember we're only friends, nothing more. To remember her words and not the feeling her hand cupping my face gave me.

I watch Essie now, the way she curls into that utter jerk, and grit my teeth. I should be happy for her. That's what a friend would do.

There's something about her posture though, something in the way she moves or the expression on her face that I can barely discern in the firelight. I'm not exactly sure what it is, but she's sad.

I know, because I know Essie. I've spent weeks hanging out with her and studying her when she isn't aware I'm watching her. I've seen her happy. I've seen her stressed and frustrated by her work. I've seen her upset after a fight with her parents or a spiked barb from David.

Jeremy says something and Essie laughs half-heartedly, her fake smile barely curving her cheeks.

I've completely forgotten about Annie right next to me until she runs a fingernail up the denim of my jeans. "I've missed you so much." She presses into me. I didn't think it was possible for her to get closer, but I was wrong. "Did you think about what I said?"

I try to clear my mind of thoughts of Essie so I can concentrate on what Annie is saying.

I see Jeremy run his hand along Essie's cheek and everything goes a little blurry.

What did Annie ask me? Have I thought about what she said. What did she say? My mind flashes back to the day in Essie's back yard. My brain automatically thinks of Essie, her cheeks flushed and eyes bright between our kisses. I shove the image away and refocus on Annie.

She wants to get back together.

I haven't thought about it because I don't want to do it. There's nothing at all to think about. It's a no-brainer. I told her that the day she came around and told me she'd made a mistake.

Apparently she didn't listen.

"I've already told you, Annie," I say, then freeze as Essie looks away from Jeremy, straight at me.

She's far enough away and the lighting is poor enough that I shouldn't be able to see the change in her expression as she takes in the sight of me, sitting here with Annie pressed against me, her leg hooked over mine. When did that happen? I've been so laser-focussed on the girl who doesn't want me, I haven't noticed this other girl throwing herself at me.

Essie looks away again and I feel like a limb has been severed.

"Listen, Annie," I say, forcing myself to look down at Annie and deal with one problem at a time. "I'm not interested in ever getting back together with you."

She pouts and her lips quivers. "But—" she starts, and I cut her off.

"There's nothing you can say that would change my mind."

I glance back at Essie, hoping thoughts of her will help

galvanise me. It doesn't help, because now she's kissing him. Her hands are resting on his hips, his hands are roaming and the moment I glance away I see one settle on Essie's leg, right below the hem of her skirt.

Déjà vu.

Annie's followed my gaze. "If you're turning me down for her, you might want to rethink it," she says.

I push aside my rage at Jeremy. I can't let this play out like last time, when I swooped in thinking I was helping. Because Essie was right. She's no damsel in distress. I should be more worried about Jeremy if he puts a foot wrong. Essie's wrath is vast.

"It's not about Essie," I say. "It's about me not wanting to go back to the girl who cheated on me. It's about me realising I'm worth more than that. So no, Annie. I'm not interested. I hope you find someone who makes you happy, but it won't be me."

I push up from the couch and stalk away, leaving Annie and Zoe dumbstruck on the couch.

The words spread through me. I hadn't planned on saying that. I wasn't sure what I would say when I opened my mouth.

But it's true.

I may really want to be loved, but not by someone who was so careless with my feelings. I'm not giving her a chance to break me again.

I said it wasn't about Essie, which isn't exactly true. It's not about me wanting to be with her, but it's still about her, because she's the one who made me see it.

She's never needed anyone else's validation to realise her own worth. She is simply as strong and wonderful as she is, regardless of anyone else's opinion. Despite everyone else's opinion.

I grab another drink and loiter near the table.

Cayley stops beside me, pouring her own drink. "That was unexpected," she says, tipping her head towards where Essie and Jeremy are still going at it.

I bristle but try to hide it beneath a shrug. No one else needs to know how much distress it's causing me.

Cayley watches me for a moment too long before turning away, and I know she's noticed. That's what happens when you've known someone your entire life. She knows everything and it's near impossible to hide anything, let alone something as big as how devastated I am by screwing up my chance with Essie, again.

Cayley makes a pained sound. "Oh, no. Jax, you should stop that."

I glance over and want to throw punches. Essie's skirt is hitched up, Jeremy's hand disappearing beneath it.

"I can't," I mutter. "She'd string me up and gut me alive."

Cayley stares at me for a moment, her mouth a grim line, then sighs. "I'll do it, then."

She takes two steps and freezes as Essie shoves Jeremy away, slapping at his hand as it re-emerges.

"I said, don't," she exclaims, her voice loud enough to carry across the space between us. It's loud, but it's low. Angry.

Jeremy leans in to say something to her, but Essie pushes him aside again, standing up.

"I was," she says, glaring down at him, "but having fun doesn't automatically mean I want to do that."

People are starting to turn and look.

"Come on, Ess. I told you I didn't want any drama." Jeremy leans back, casual as anything.

"If you didn't want drama," she shouts at him, "you shouldn't have kept trying to put your hand up my skirt when I repeatedly told you not to!"

Pride glows in my heart.

Damsel in distress she is not.

"Oh come off it, Essie, you told me you wanted to have fun but didn't want any drama. All you *are* is drama."

Essie recoils and I start forward, ready to come to her defence whether she wants it or not.

Jeremy gestures around. "Just look at the scene you're causing."

Essie glances up and looks around. Too many people are watching this unfold. Her expression closes down, stripping the rage and defiance away, leaving her face devoid of any emotion.

Her gaze lands on me again for the briefest second, then she spins away and rushes into the darkness.

Chapter Forty-Three

ESSIE

THE SOUNDS of the party fade behind me as the darkness swallows me up. I stumble, but manage to keep my feet under me. My vision is blurring and it's hard to see where I'm stepping.

I search the indistinct dark shapes until I recognise Jax's car, sliding down into the grass beside it.

Jax was right. I knew that all the way back at Melissa's party. That what Jeremy did wasn't okay, and I let him anyway because I didn't want to cause any drama. I didn't want to cause a scene or have people talking about me.

So many people look at me and assume confidence. And a lot of the time I have it. But it's still a constant battle between figuring out who I want to be, and what other people expect me to be. My parents want me to fit into their "ideal daughter" mould with a steady, mindless job. Society as a whole wants me to be small, fitting into the tiny box allowed for me.

No one's ever celebrated me for my differences, for standing out and loving myself and being passionate about what I want to do with my life. For being a little different.

No.

The world wants me to be insignificant, to blend in like everyone else.

And now I *have* stood up for myself … and caused drama and a huge scene that I've been trying all along to avoid.

Everyone saw.

Everyone.

Including Jax.

The whole night has been a disaster, from dancing with Jax to overhearing Annie talking about him, to Jeremy appearing out of the blue, his hands sliding around my waist from behind.

I went along with it. It's not the first time he's held me like that, and it seemed easier than whatever was going to happen next with Jax. Either we were going to ignore it, or he was going to want to talk about it and hash out my embarrassment over thinking something was going to happen. I didn't want to do either.

Jeremy was there and it was easy, and though he doesn't make my blood burn like Jax does, kissing him isn't bad.

He makes me feel soft, makes my insides melt, and I want to curl into him and be cared for.

But his damn wandering hands, asking for more. Always asking for more.

It meant I couldn't be soft anymore. Not after I'd realised the difference between kissing Jax and kissing Jeremy.

I was never nervous of Jax's hands. I didn't ever hesitate when he touched me. I knew I was safe with him.

With Jax, I was strong, not soft.

A shadow emerges from the darkness and I scramble to my feet, hastily brushing tears off my face.

I'm expecting Jeremy.

I'm expecting Brooke.

I am not expecting Jax.

"Estella," he breathes.

I don't know what to say to him. So I say nothing. There isn't anything I can say that can adequately cover everything that has happened tonight.

"Are you okay?" he asks, stepping close.

"Yeah, fine," I say.

He taps something on his phone, then slides it into his pocket. "Are you sure?" He reaches a hand towards me and it hangs in the air between us. I shift away and he lets it drop.

"I said I'm fine," I bite out, turning and leaning my hip against the side of the car.

"You can talk to me," he says, and I know he's moved to stand beside me, but far enough away that I can't *feel* him. "If you want to, you know you can talk to me, right? We are friends, after all." There's a little smile in his voice as he echoes back my words from earlier tonight – before everything went wrong.

"Yeah, sure," I say.

"Estella." His hand rests on my shoulder, big and warm and solid. I used to think that meant I was safe with him, but after hearing what Annie said, I don't think that anymore.

"Hey, he's not worth getting upset over." He tries to turn me with gentle pressure, but I resist.

"I'm not upset over that," I mutter.

"Then what is it?" His hand softens and he moves in closer. Now I can feel the heat of him. "Is it about before you saw him?"

"Look," I say, spinning to face him so abruptly his hand

falls away. "It's fine, okay? You don't need to pretend you care. I get it. I'm just David's over-dramatic little brat of a sister. I'm childish and throw tantrums and even the idea of us being anything more than whatever we were when you moved in is gross, okay? I get it. You don't have to worry about it."

"Essie," he gasps, and I flinch at the use of my nickname. It's not the first time tonight he's used it, either. I hate it when he calls me Estella. I hate it even more when he doesn't. "What the … Where did *that* come from?"

"I heard you, and then I heard what you've been telling everyone else about me."

"I have no idea what you're talking about." He's raising his voice now, frustration or anger, or both, evident in it.

"I heard Annie talking about me. How you'd told her I was over-dramatic and prone to tantrums and 'all a bit much'," I snap. My voice wavers across the words and my eyes grow hot.

"What? I *never* said that to her. I've never said anything like it," he shouts back. "Did you think maybe you should talk to *me* after overhearing some random conversation that had nothing to do with me or something I said, or did you decide to jump straight into the drama?"

"I heard you talking to David about me," I cry, his words flinging salt into already stinging wounds. "The day you moved in. I believe your words were 'She's your kid sister, eww'. I'd forgotten about it, what with you appearing to be an actual decent human, and that time you kissed me."

He gapes at me, opening and closing his mouth, wanting to speak but not knowing what to say.

"I still don't understand why you even did that," I say, the words pouring from me in an uncontrollable stream.

"Did what?" He drops his voice low. It's rough like it hurts to speak.

"Kissed me," I hiss back at him.

He closes his eyes for a moment, hand curling into a fist at his side like he's trying to control himself. "I kissed you," he says, voice a low rumble that absolutely, most definitely, does not send goosebumps skittering across my skin, "because I wanted to."

"So you thought you'd kiss me and push me aside like you have everyone else. Because you know what, Jackson Sherwood, you told me all those girls left you, and maybe they did, who knows, but I bet before anyone could get close to you, you tossed them aside. Like you just did to me."

"Oh come on, Estella, that's a bit much, even from you."

Chapter Forty-Four

JAX

I CANNOT BELIEVE what I said.

This whole conversation – fight, screaming match, whatever it is – has spiralled out of control so fast I don't even know what we're arguing about.

I cannot believe I accused her of jumping straight to the drama. I can't believe I said it was a bit much, even for her.

I came after her because I wanted to check that she was okay. Cayley and I split up and went looking for her. I texted Cayley once I found Essie so she could stop looking.

The tear tracks streaking Essie's face made me want to go back and give Jeremy a serious dose of consequences, and at the same time wrap her up in my arms so tightly that no one could ever hurt her again.

And then I opened my fat mouth and hurt her myself.

"I want to go home," she says now, her voice a hoarse whisper. "I'll go and find Brooke."

"Cayley will make sure she gets home," I say, voice gruff. I unlock the car and pull out my phone again, sending a text to Cayley asking her to do exactly that. Essie is in the car before

Cayley's reply comes through a moment later, confirming that Brooke will get home safely.

I slide into the driver's seat and start the engine. "Es," I say, planning to somehow apologise for all the things I've said, to somehow pull this back from the edge.

If only I could take it all back to that moment when she was leaning into me, telling me to smile because dancing with her shouldn't be so bad. When I was struggling to hold myself together as all I could think about was kissing her again. I don't know why I fought that feeling.

"Don't," Essie cuts me off before I can even get her full name out. "I don't want to talk to you. Just take me home, please."

I reverse out of the parking spot and pull onto the quiet road. There're no cars about. Everyone is preparing to count down to the New Year; to kiss at midnight and make resolutions that will last all of two weeks, despite their enthusiasm to do better in the coming year.

The radio is playing low and Essie spends the ride with her head leaning against the window, getting as far away from me as physically possible. She's totally silent, not even singing along to songs under her breath. It's so un-Essie-like and I'd do anything to hear her attempting to sing right now.

I turn into the driveway at home and she opens her door before I've turned the car off. I'm not ready for tonight to end. I can't let it end like this.

"Estella, please," I say, voice pleading. "Please talk to me."

"No, Jax." She leans back into the car and I watch as a tear glides down her cheek. Her makeup is smudged, the ponytail holding up the top part of her hair is wilted and one of the shoulder bows on her dress is crooked. "I don't want to talk to you. Not now, not ever. Go back to your life where I was simply David's kid sister who you'd never contemplate wanting anything to do with and I'll go back to thinking you're a huge jerk."

"I don't want that, Es," I say as I clench my hands around the steering wheel, knuckles turning white.

"Too bad, Jax," she says, her voice resigned. I flinch as she uses that stupid name again. "I don't want *anything* to do with you ever again." Then she shuts the car door firmly but quietly and marches into the house, her skirt swirling in her wake.

I lay my head on the steering wheel and think about what she said.

She thinks I throw people away before they get the chance to leave me. I wonder if she's right, or if she only wanted to say something mean, or maybe she wasn't even sure what she was saying and she blurted out the first words that came to mind.

It does hurt, though. It cuts me deep down, making my heart ache.

I can't tell if the pain is from what she said about other people, or if it's about not wanting to have anything to do with me ever again.

Either way, she's made it clear that whatever I'd hoped might happen between us is definitely not going to.

I climb out of the car and let myself into the house. It's completely silent. It's so eerie.

I pause in the kitchen and pick up the recipe book Miriam gave me for Christmas.

Taking it with me, I head to my room and begin to pack.

Chapter Forty-Five

ESSIE

I WAKE to the sound of car doors slamming.

I peer out my window, wondering who would be making so much noise this early on New Year's Day.

It's Jax.

He picks up a box and shoves it into the back of his car, jamming it in alongside several others. David is standing beside him, leaning on the car as Jax rearranges things to fit then tosses in another bag.

I crack my window open, hoping I'll be able to hear what they're saying.

"I still don't get why you're going," David says.

Jax slams the car door and sighs. "Because it's time I did, all right. I really appreciate you guys letting me crash here, but I've got to go."

"Is this something to do with Essie?"

"What?" Jax jerks at the mention of my name and his eyes flicker to my window. Luckily I'm standing far enough back that he shouldn't be able to see me. "Why would you think it's anything to do with her?"

David shrugs. "I dunno. Because it's Essie."

"Dude," Jax says, "she's your sister and she's really not that bad. Try being nice to her occasionally, all right? You might be surprised how fun she is."

David says nothing but I think I can make out his sceptical expression. "Yeah, unlikely," he finally says. "But you aren't leaving because of something she did?"

"No," Jax says, exasperation colouring his voice. "Essie's fine, okay? Let it go. I found a new place to stay and I figured I'd get out of your way."

"You know this means I have to go back to eating Essie's cooking though, right?"

Jax laughs. "Maybe she's learnt something from me and you'll be lucky."

"Maybe, but I doubt it," David says, then gives Jax a gentle punch on the arm. "Catch you round, man."

Jax grins, but it's hollow. He looks ragged, jaw rough with stubble, eyes tired, the collar of his jacket folded under.

My eyes linger on that jacket as I remember the night at the beach, when he let me wear it home. The leather was so soft and smelled like him. It was still warm, even after it had been sitting on the beach while we swam. I didn't know it then, but it was almost like being hugged by him.

Almost, because nothing can quite compare to the real thing.

Which I guess is something I'll never get again. Not after what I said.

David heads inside while Jax pulls out of the driveway and I collapse back into bed, pulling the covers over my head.

I should get up, shower, brush my teeth and eat some food.

I should sew the dresses I have on order, finish the detail stitches on Melissa's and Cayley's bridesmaid dresses.

Instead I stay in bed, curled under the covers, and spend my day intermittently sobbing and napping.

Mum forces me downstairs at dinner time and I sit sullenly at the table, picking at my food, staring at the empty seat across the table.

When the meal is over and I've cleared the table I head straight back to my room.

David intercepts me at the top of the stairs. "What happened last night?"

"Nothing," I mutter, trying to step around him.

"Come on, Essie. What happened at the party?"

I stare at him.

He knows. How does he know? I heard Jax tell him he'd found somewhere else to live and that him leaving was nothing to do with me.

"Nothing happened," I say again.

"Ess." He lays a hand on my arm to stop me running past him and slamming my door. I glance up at him, shocked that he's called me Ess, somewhat endearingly. "I heard about Jeremy."

"Oh," is all I can manage. I've mostly forgotten about it. Well, I haven't. I've been really good at blanking it out though; the way his hand felt skimming up the skin of my thigh. I suppress a shudder.

"Are you okay?"

"What?" I ask, dumbstruck. David's never been the caring type. I don't think he really knows how to handle emotions, and with me having so many of them I'm not sure he's ever known how to handle me.

"Are you okay? After what Jeremy did?"

"I – uh, yeah. I'm all right," I say, and to my horror my eyes start to burn as tears well.

David's face goes blank with panic as he notices my tears and I let out a choked sound that's both hysterical laughing and a sob. "Your face," I gasp, the hysterical laughing and sobbing continuing. "It's fine, David. Really, I'm okay about it."

"Then why exactly are you crying?"

I sigh and wipe at my tears, leaning heavily against the wall as emotional exhaustion washes over me. "Everyone saw it," I say, my voice small. "Everyone saw me make this huge stupid scene and I'm so embarrassed."

The shame washes over me again.

The shame of letting a guy near me after I'd asked him to stop and he kept pushing. I should never have let Jeremy near me after the first time. He didn't try anything the other times I saw him, but I should have known better.

The shame of blowing up and yelling at him in front of everyone, for saying hideous things to Jax when he came to check on me.

"Ess," David says, leaning against the wall and facing me. "Yeah, a lot of people saw. And you know what? They all think you're an absolute boss for putting him in his place."

"What?" I hear the words but they're not sinking in. There's no way people could have said that. I was stupid, and David must be joking, but for once his expression isn't laced with derision and sarcasm.

"Jeremy's a bit of a dick. Honestly, I don't know why any of us are really friends with him. And he's been known to push the boundaries before. Cayley told me he's done it to someone else. He pushed and pushed and the girl didn't know how to stop it. Cay told me what you did. She's so proud of you. So are a lot of other people. They're impressed, Essie. For what it's worth, so am I." He pauses for a moment and rubs the back of his neck. "Not that I should be surprised. You don't take crap from anyone."

I stare at him. People are impressed with me. I can't quite process it all.

I wonder if Jax is proud of me too.

I don't think so. Maybe for a second he was, but not after he came to find me and I screamed at him. I may not have overreacted with Jeremy, but I sure did with Jax. He was right. I should have asked him first, talked to him.

"David," I say. He's started turning away to head back down the hall but stops at my words. "Did Jax ever say anything mean about me?"

His eyes narrow, growing flinty as they take in my tears, the hair I haven't bothered to brush today. "He never, ever said anything mean about you to me, but if he said anything like that to you, I'll kick his ass," he says.

"No," I say, "no, no. He didn't. I overheard Annie talking about me and I assumed Jax had said what she was saying. Would he? Could it have been him?"

David shakes his head slowly, letting out a long breath. "It wasn't him, Ess. He's barely spoken to Annie since they split up. Only that day she came here and he sent her packing. She came crying to me after that." He rubs the back of his neck again and lets out a big sigh. "Essie, I'm sorry. Whatever you heard … it was probably from me. Anything Jax said about you, it would have been good."

Chapter Forty-Six

JAX

I STARE up at the ceiling, lit golden by the tiny fairy lights Cayley has strung throughout her room.

I shift and the air mattress I'm on squeaks beneath me.

I sigh.

The sofa bed at David's – Essie's – I don't know how to refer to it anymore – wasn't great, but this air mattress will be the end of me.

I lied to David when I left. I hadn't found a place to stay. Instead, I turned up on Aunt Kate's doorstep. She took one look at me and told Cayley to find the mattress.

No one has questioned why I'm here. Melissa, Cayley and Kate have simply accepted that I am, though I assume Cayley has a fairly good idea.

I go to work, I help cook dinner, I lie here and stare at Cayley's ceiling and through all of it, despite my best efforts, I think about Essie.

I think about all those little moments, the snippets of herself she showed me as she gradually let her guard down around me, when every tiny positive interaction felt like a reward.

I think about how she heard David and I talking the day I moved in. I can't remember the conversation. I assume she heard David warning me not to flirt with her and whatever stupid response I gave.

I hate that she heard it. I hate that she thinks I'd ever say anything about her that isn't describing exactly how perfect she is.

It's no wonder she hated me at the start, after whatever it was I said. Something about me calling her David's kid sister.

The thing I can't understand is why I said that. I've always liked Essie. I've always thought she was fun and interesting, and loved that she didn't take crap from anyone.

People have been talking about her in the past few days, about what happened at the party with Jeremy. Every single person has applauded her bravery. But I don't think Essie sees it that way.

Essie doesn't want to be the centre of attention. She doesn't want to cause any drama.

Essie wants to be herself.

But she thinks she can't be, so she'd rather be small so she can fit into the world around her.

I hate it.

She doesn't realise the world will always grow around her.

I remember the evening on the beach, first when she listened to all my woes, then how her face lit up as she raced for the water.

I remember the night of Melissa's party when her eyes flashed with fury at me, the day outside her bedroom when I apologised for moving into her space. I remember the day in the kitchen when I kissed her, again and again.

I groan and roll over, the mattress moving awkwardly under me.

"Jax," Cayley mutters from her bed, "are you all right?"

"Yeah," I say, "sorry."

I try to lie still, to not disturb Cayley. Kate was apologetic when she said I'd have to sleep here. The spare room where I'd normally sleep was still filled with wedding supplies, which was the original reason I didn't stay here when I moved out of the flat. Cayley doesn't mind sharing, but I am also acutely aware of how annoying I am being.

Forcing myself to lie still makes me want to fidget more, and I endure it as long as I can before turning again.

Cayley sits up and flicks on a dim light.

"Jax, what's up?"

I blink at the sudden change in light, turning to face my cousin as she peers down at me, her long hair pulled into a loose bun on top of her head, reminding me again of Essie.

"Nothing," I say. "Sorry."

"Stop saying you're sorry and tell me why you've been sleeping on my floor for a week."

A week? Has it been that long already? The days are all blurring together as I wander through them in a daze. I can't even focus on my course work. Every time I pick up one of the workbooks, I think about sitting across from Essie while I worked and she sewed.

I don't say anything, so Cayley speaks again. "What happened with Essie?"

"What?" My gaze cuts to her, and I realise my reaction has

given me away. I slump back down onto the mattress. "We had a fight. At New Year's."

"Well, that much was kind of obvious," she says. "What happened?"

I sigh, the sound echoing through the room as I gather my thoughts.

"She was upset over Jeremy and also because she thought I'd said some awful stuff to Annie about her." Another gusty breath. "She said things, I said things. I took her home. She told me she never wants to see me again."

"Did you say awful things to Annie about her?"

"What? No! Of course not."

"Okay," Cayley says, raising her hands in a *calm down* gesture. "I'm just getting my facts straight. Why does she think you did?"

"She overheard Annie talking about her." I wince. I cannot imagine that would have been nice to overhear. Since we broke up I've realised how petty Annie can be, though I never noticed it while we were together. Hindsight's such a wonderful thing.

"How does she even know who Annie is?" Cayley's face is thoughtful. "She wouldn't have met her before, would she?"

"Yeah, she has." I pause and gather my thoughts. I want to be careful I don't give away a second of what happened before Annie arrived that day. "Annie came by one day. I had no idea she even knew where I was. But she wanted to get back together. I said no."

"Does Essie know you said no?"

"Umm …" I think and think, wracking my brains for any mention of Annie after that day. "I don't think so," I say eventually. "We never really talked about her after that."

"You'd talked about her before?"

"Geez," I say tossing my pillow at her, "what's with the inquisition?"

"I'm only trying to get the full picture," she says.

"Fine," I grumble. "Yes, we'd talked about her before. We – I'd told her about the breakup."

"Seriously?" Cayley's incredulous. "You haven't even told me about the breakup."

I shrug. "I – It wasn't really intentional."

"You guys are friends, yeah?"

"Yeah. Well, we were." I fiddle with the edge of the blanket, unable to meet Cayley's eyes. I don't want to see the expression on her face, whether it's pity or anything else. I don't want to know.

Cayley slides out of bed, landing beside me on the air mattress and leaning against the wall. I prop myself up next to her.

"Don't bite my head off for asking this, but were you anything else?"

"What do you mean?" I know exactly what she means.

"You know exactly what I mean."

I huff a little laugh as my thoughts and her words overlap. "Yes," I breathe, not wanting to acknowledge it. I wish I could simply bury it all.

"Did anything happen between you? Do you know if she likes you too?"

Heat finds the back of my neck and my palms feel sweaty. I rub them against my thigh.

"I kissed her."

Cayley gasps but gestures eagerly for me to continue. "Like at first she hated me … then slowly she started to not hate me.

I liked her even when she still hated me. I couldn't help it. She's just so …" I can't find the words to describe her. I wave my hands in the air while I struggle to find the right words.

"I know," Cayley says. "I know what you mean."

I nod. "We ended up hanging out. She started not hating me so much and we became friends, I guess. Then one day I kissed her." I exhale, then take another shaking breath. "That was the day Annie showed up." I drop my head back and it bangs lightly against the wall. I feel like doing it again, but harder. "She wouldn't talk about it again."

"She kissed you back?" Cayley finds my hand and wraps it up in both of her small, soft, warm ones. She doesn't seem to mind the clamminess.

"Yeah," I say, squeezing her hands tight. "It was the greatest moment of my life."

Cayley chuckles and rests her head on my shoulder. It's so much like the night on the beach. My heart clenches tight.

"Jax," Cayley says, lifting her head to peer up at me, "why aren't you fighting for her?"

"What do you mean?"

"I mean, why are you walking away? Why aren't you apologising, asking her to take you back? Why aren't you fighting for her?"

"Because she doesn't want me to. Remember, the whole 'I never want to see you again' thing?"

"She was hurt, Jax, and so were you. I know you find it hard to let people in, but …" she releases a heavy breath "… sometimes you have to fight for them, instead of letting them walk away."

I sit, stunned and silent, while Cayley wraps her arms around me. Her words echo through my brain, lining up alongside the ones Essie threw at me about tossing people aside before they can leave me.

"What if she doesn't want me? What if she still walks away?" The words come out choked, and shame at my weakness rolls through me.

"She might, Jax, but you'll never know if you don't at least try."

Chapter Forty-Seven

ESSIE

CAYLEY AND MELISSA look completely gorgeous in their bridesmaid dresses. Kate cries as the sisters stand side by side in front of a floor-length mirror in her bedroom.

The lilac satin bodices fit the curves of their bodies perfectly and the chiffon overskirts float delicately to the floor. Two slim, but not shoestring, straps start on each side of the front of the bodices, working their way over the shoulders and criss-crossing to tie off in delicate bows in the centre of the girls' backs.

Tiny delicate beaded motifs are scattered along the neckline and waist of the dresses, tendrils dripping down into the skirts.

"Oh my God, Essie," Melissa says. "They're so pretty."

"They're perfect," Kate says, wiping at her tears. "Go get out of them before I cry on them."

Melissa laughs, squeezes me in a quick hug and leaves the room. Kate follows her to help with the straps.

"How're you doing, Essie?" Cayley asks, hanging behind.

"Oh, um, I'm fine," I say, surprised.

"You're okay after everything with Jeremy?"

"Yeah, fine," I say again. The embarrassment is still hot and awful whenever I remember that night, but most of the time it's not that part of the night that I remember. It's less about Jeremy's lazy drawl about me making a scene, and more about Jax's hazel eyes, wide in confusion or squeezing shut every time I said something awful.

"And about Jax?"

"What?" I stop fiddling with the dress bag I've been using to avoid eye contact with Cayley while tears prickle at the back of my eyes. "Did he put you up to this?"

"No, of course not. Why would you say that?"

I sigh and shove the bag away. "I don't know, because … because …" I shrug. "I don't know why. Because he's a jerk."

Oh, the anger is back. It's been the most surprising part of my heartbreak. The sadness I was expecting; the loneliness – yeah, sure, but the anger was a total surprise. I can swing from the depths of sadness to a furious rage in the blink of an eye. I go from hating myself for hurting him to hating him for hurting me.

"Oh, honey." Cayley takes my hands in hers. "He's really not. I know he hurt you, but he cares about you. He just doesn't know how to deal with that." She squeezes my hands and I stare at her, dumbstruck. "I know he's got some sort of reputation with some girls in your year, but Jax has never screwed anyone around. He's never led them on, he's never pushed them further than where they want to go. Everyone has always known where they stand with him. He's as straight up as they come, if a little daft about all this kind of thing."

Her words bite. The ones about Jax never pushing further than where a girl wants to go.

"I've never known where I've stood with him," I mutter.

"Haven't you?" she asks.

"Well, he mocked me relentlessly, was a total jerk, then started being not-so-awful for a little while before he turned into a jerk again. So, no. I don't know where I stand. And what you said before, that he cares about me … no. Just no."

"Why?"

"Because he wouldn't. I'm his best mate's gross kid sister. I heard him say it."

"Did you ever consider he was simply telling David what he wanted to hear? And that maybe it was before he even spent any time with you and he realised you were more than his best friend's little sister?"

"How could you possibly know that?" I laugh, a harsh bitter sound.

"Because he told me. He lay on my bedroom floor and told me everything, from David saying he could stay as long as he didn't hit on you, to all the times you hung out, to how amazing he thinks you are, to how he screwed it all up."

"He did not."

"He did, and I know we've talked before about how talking about his feelings doesn't come easily to Jax. But you can ask him yourself. He should be home soon."

"What?"

Cayley sighs. "I wasn't supposed to say anything. But where did you think he went?"

"He told David he got himself a new flat."

Cayley snorts. "Yeah, my bedroom floor. He's …" She pauses, and looks as though she might not finish the sentence. She meets my gaze, takes a deep breath and continues. "He's not very good with the sticking around part. He thinks it's easier to walk away. I think mostly he's scared to fight for someone in case they still don't want him. Too many people have walked away from him. But Essie, we all know you're worth fighting for."

I stand there shaking my head, trying to align everything she's said with how it's all played out.

She can't be right.

"He's going to kick my butt for telling you," she says, smiling at me. "But I think it was worth it."

"I'm not going to tell him. I'm not going to say anything to him."

"You should, Essie. You should talk to him."

I shake my head. "Thank you, but no. I need to go," I say, desperate to be long gone before Jax arrives home. He traded a sofa bed in our spare room for a mattress on the floor of his cousin's bedroom.

"You'll be here on Saturday though, right?" Cayley's face is serious. "Whatever you've got going on with Jax, please make sure you come Saturday."

I nod. The wedding. "I'll be there," I say as she pulls me into a hug. I resist for a moment, then let myself be wrapped up in her arms.

"The dresses are beautiful, Essie," she whispers in my ear. "Promise you'll think about what I said."

Chapter Forty-Eight

JAX

I SIT in my car outside work and debate with myself.

Cayley told me Essie would be going round for a dress fitting this afternoon.

Am I rushing home in the hopes I'll see Essie and can get on my knees and beg her to let me make it up to her?

Or am I sitting here for a while longer, making sure she's gone before I make it home so I don't have to see what outfit she's wearing today, if her hair is up in those two buns on the top of her head, what colour her nails are, if she's wearing that pink lipstick I may have dreamt about on more than one occasion?

I think about what Cayley said, about trying, about fighting for her. Sadly, she's right. I've never fought for anyone. Every single time I've let them walk away. If they've come back to me I've turned them away again because I've been unable to get past the hurt. I haven't been able to trust that I won't be dropped again.

But Essie … she makes me want to.

I start the car and slam it into gear, a little more enthusiastically than anticipated, and wince as the gearbox crunches.

Someone is on my side because I hit no traffic and no red lights, reaching Aunt Kate's house in record time.

Essie's car is still in the driveway and I exhale, slumping onto the steering wheel in relief.

I park and climb out, taking deep, steadying breaths. I push open the front door and there she is, reaching for the door herself.

She freezes at the sight of me, her mouth dropped open into a soft 'o'.

"Estella," I manage to say after a moment of simply staring. Her name slides from my mouth like it's the only word I was meant to say. Her eyes flutter closed as the l's roll off my tongue.

She's wearing black exercise shorts and a black t-shirt. Her hair is in a simple, slightly messy ponytail low on her head, her nail polish is chipped and there's not a trace of that pink lipstick. She doesn't appear to be wearing makeup at all. Her eyes are lined with red and she looks pale. Even the vivid green of her eyes looks washed out.

She's Essie, but also she isn't. It's like a watered-down version of her. I don't think I've ever seen her wear black before. Her hair isn't even pulled up high on her head. The overall effect looks … defeated.

My heart splinters. Is this because of me? Is this my fault, this vague outline of the girl I've always admired for her vivaciousness?

"Estella," I say again, at a loss for what else to say, for how to apologise and explain and beg her not to hate me again. "I'm—"

"No," she cuts me off. "I have to go." Her voice is shaky, verging on breaking.

"Please." I try again, my voice coming out sad and pitiful.

She pushes past me, out into the sunshine and to her car.

I follow her. I want to stop her from going, I want to reach out and put my palm against her arm, loop my fingers around her wrist and pull her to me so I can wrap my arms around her and feel her nestle her face against my neck. I ache with the longing.

But the touching has been a thing from the start, and I know right now there is zero percent chance she wants me to. I won't push it.

"Can we talk for a minute, Estella?"

"I don't think that's a good idea," she says, her voice low and barely audible over the sound of a vehicle on the road behind the fence.

She climbs into her car and I manage to grab the door before she can close it. "Please." My voice cracks, the same way my heart is. There's a twisting pain in my gut that's wrenching a hole there, bigger and bigger each time she avoids my eyes.

"Let me go, Jax." Her voice is tired, sad. There's no sobbing or shouting, only resignation and a single tear that trickles down her cheek.

"I don't want to let you go," I say, not only talking about this moment.

Her eyes finally meet mine and another tear spills over. Her bottom lip trembles. I hold my hand out to her and her gaze follows it. All she has to do is take it. She watches my hand, my face. I don't let myself look anywhere else but at her.

She takes a deep breath.

"Jax!" A voice cuts through the moment and Essie jerks as though she's waking up with a start.

She rips her gaze away and I glance wildly around for the source of that oh-so-familiar voice.

My mother is standing in the middle of the driveway, suitcase beside her. "Surprise!"

I stare at her. I've been spending way too much time lately staring at people in shock. "You're here! I mean, obviously, yes. Why? You never said you were coming back."

I find myself stumbling away from Essie's car and Mum meets me, wrapping me up in a hug.

"I wasn't going to miss my sister's wedding," she says with a grin. There are tears in her eyes as she looks up at me. "Look how you've grown."

I laugh and roll my eyes. "I really haven't. I've missed you, though."

"Oh, I've missed you too. You'll never know how much."

Dimly, I register the sound of the car door closing and the engine starting.

Essie.

I pull away from Mum and turn back to the car, which is now halfway out the driveway. "Essie," I call. I break into a run. I should be able to catch her before she hits the road. "Essie!" I shout, louder this time.

She doesn't stop. She pulls into the road and accelerates, disappearing around the corner.

I'm left standing on the footpath, breath coming in short gasps as I try to not let my heart shatter completely.

Chapter Forty-Nine

ESSIE

I'M LYING face-down on my bed when there's a knock at my door.

"Yeah?" I call out, the sound muffled by the blankets my face is buried in.

"Essie?" Mum opens the door a crack, hesitating.

"Yeah." I roll over and wave her in.

She perches on the edge of my bed, looking nervous, like one loud noise could send her running. It's an unusual look on her.

The rest of her looks the same as usual: sensible jeans, practical t-shirt, her hair, the same colour as mine, pulled back in its typical braid.

"What's up?" I ask while staring at the ceiling.

"Why don't you tell me?" she says, her voice soft. I cut my gaze to her. She's fiddling with a fold in the blanket while staring around my room like she's never seen it before.

"What do you mean?" My hackles are beginning to rise, even though I'm exhausted and really have no interest in fighting with her.

"I mean …" She pauses, softening her voice again. Apparently she can't help but fight with me either. "I mean, you've been shut in here since New Year and you don't quite seem yourself."

"I'm fine," I mutter. *Don't quite seem yourself* is like the understatement of the year. I can't find myself, or I don't know who I am anymore. Everything feels hollow.

I managed to finish the dresses for Cayley and Melissa, and luckily I've caught up on most of my other orders and there isn't anything too pressing to do, because I don't want to look at my sewing machine, let alone make things on it.

I tried to find something cute to wear when I delivered the dresses earlier, but everything I pulled out of my wardrobe made me feel uncomfortable. There was nothing that made me feel good. So I stayed in the shorts and t-shirt I was already in. The thought of applying makeup was simply too much, so I went barefaced.

"I thought you might be happy about that," I mutter, turning my face away so she doesn't see the tears welling up.

"Essie." Her voice is a breathy whisper and her hand settles gently on my shoulder. "Why would you say that?"

"Because it's no secret that who I am is not exactly the child you wanted. And I get it," I say, rushing the words out.

"That's … that's not true at all, Essie," she says, voice full of shock. I can't look at her, can't bear to turn and see her face. Instead my gaze rests on the half-finished pink dress I've been slowly working on for the past month.

The thing is, it's true. My parents wanted another child like David, who kept his head down and was good at school and got a sensible job and didn't charge through life in a blur of chaos and colour and noise.

I could handle them not being able to cope with all of me, but New Year made me realise it's not only them I'm too much for.

It's everyone.

It's Jax.

I think of him when he burst through the front door at his aunt's house and stopped dead at the sight of me.

His hair was sticking up like he'd been running his hands through it, his jaw was rough with stubble and his eyes were tired. He looked a mess, a little like how I felt.

I wanted nothing more than to wrap my arms around him and make him feel better, but I know it wouldn't have done that.

Did you think maybe you should talk to me … or did you decide to jump straight into the drama?

I shove thoughts of Jax away, but it's too late. The tears spill over and race down the sides of my face, dripping onto the bed.

"Oh Essie," Mum says, then her weight shifts. I expect her to leave the room and leave her over-dramatic daughter to it, but she doesn't. She lies down right beside me, squishing herself onto the mattress. "I'm sorry," she says, and I almost fall over the side of the bed.

"What?" My voice is a hoarse croak.

She sighs and her hand finds mine, giving it a little squeeze. "When you were born, I was so excited to have a little girl. Don't start on the 'gender is irrelevant' conversation, Ess. Let me finish."

I bite my tongue.

"Anyway," she continues, "I used to sit on the back porch with you every night while David played outside. He loved that time at twilight when everything was fading." She shakes her head like she doesn't understand, and I find myself stifling a little laugh. "I used to sit there with you in my arms and wish on the first star."

"Wait, like the whole 'starlight, starbright' thing?" I remember her telling me about the first star when I was little, when we'd sit on that back porch and drink hot chocolate when the summer nights started getting cool.

"Yes, the whole 'starlight, starbright' thing. I used to wish every night that my little girl would grow up to be brave and bold and not let a single person ever tell her she couldn't do something. I wished that she'd learn to stick up for herself and fight for others who couldn't fight for themselves and have all her dreams come true."

I have to wipe the tears away now, before they drown me. They're pouring down my face, unstoppable torrents. I try to speak but Mum continues.

"And I'm sorry Essie, because all of my wishes came true, and I didn't notice. I got too caught up in what society expects from people and what we're supposed to be doing and I was worried that other people weren't ready for someone as brave and special as you. I'm sorry I ever made you feel less than amazing, but I want you to know I'm very, very proud of you."

I sniff and wipe more tears from my face. I can't speak, though. I don't know what to say to that. Will there ever be words to respond to that?

"I spoke to David," she says after a few moments of silence. "He told me a little of what happened at that party, where you put that boy in his place."

I cringe. The memory itself is awful. The way Jeremy gave

me that lazy smile and drawled about me causing a scene. It makes my skin prickle with rage and shame.

"I'm extremely proud of you for that," she says.

"You shouldn't be," I mutter. "I should have known better. I'd been warned."

"I'm proud regardless. Your brother is too."

I laugh, and the sound is so loud it startles us both.

"I also spoke to Jax."

My laugh dies and silence hangs in the air between us. "Yeah?" I say eventually.

"The day he left. He wanted to thank me for letting him stay. He also told me I should talk to you about your business, because that's what it is. Not just a hobby, not something to pass the time, but a business."

"Well, yeah," I say. "It is."

"I'd really like to hear about it sometime, if you'd like to share with me." She squeezes my hand again. I'd forgotten she was holding it and warmth floods through me. "He was rather adamant about how incredible you are, Essie."

I close my eyes and cringe. "Don't, Mum."

She nudges me with her shoulder, but thankfully changes the subject. "How's the dress coming?"

I shrug, awkwardly while lying down. "Not great."

"Aren't you going to wear it to the wedding on Saturday?"

"I don't think I'm going to go to the wedding," I say, rolling onto my side, away from her.

"Why not, Ess?"

"Because …" I take a deep breath, fully prepared for this line of conversation to go very, very wrong. "Because I was awful to Jax and it's supposed to be a happy day for him and his family. I hurt him and I don't want to see him because I think he broke my heart too." My voice cracks and breaks.

The sobs come now, wracking my body, leaving me shuddering. Mum wraps her arm around me, pulling me tight against her. "Oh Ess, have you spoken to him? Like properly had a conversation?"

"No," I say between hiccupping breaths. "I saw him today, though."

"How was he?"

"He looked awful," I say, and another wave of tears hits me and she squeezes me tight.

"Do you want to go to the wedding? If Jax wasn't there, would you want to go?"

"Yes," I say, the answer coming immediately. I desperately want to see my dresses as part of the wedding. I want to celebrate with Melissa when her stepdad becomes an official, legal part of her family. I want to dance with Cayley because she is so much fun and so kind.

"Then go. Don't let a boy stop you from doing that. But Essie, I would suggest you speak with him at some point, maybe after the wedding. The two of you were special to each other, we could all see it. Don't throw it away without trying."

"I thought I wasn't allowed a boyfriend," I say.

Mum sighs. "That was unfair of me," she says after a moment's hesitation. "I thought I was helping, protecting you. I forgot that you're old enough and brave enough and strong enough to protect yourself. And Jax … well, he's a good one."

"I'll think about it," I whisper. "Though I still don't think I'll have time to finish the dress."

"If you had help, could you do it?"

"Maybe. I don't know."

"Shall we try?" She pushes herself off the bed and picks up the dress, holding it out to me. A peace offering.

I swipe at my cheeks again, removing the last of the tears, and stand. "Yeah, we can try," I say, sceptical but glad she wants to try.

Chapter Fifty

JAX

MUM'S ARRIVAL sets off the chaos that is preparing for a wedding.

Kate fought hard to have a simple wedding in their own backyard, but Cayley, Melissa and Travis managed to convince her to hold it at a professional venue. Which I am extremely relieved about, because I can only imagine the level of work that would be involved if we'd had to do everything ourselves.

For the next two days, any second that I'm not asleep or working I'm running wedding-related errands. I've even taken time off to get ready for this. I pick up my suit, deliver bits and pieces to the venue and tackle a myriad of other tiny tasks. The worst one was transporting the wedding cake from the baker to the venue late on Friday afternoon.

I settle it safely onto the venue's kitchen bench and heave a huge sigh of relief.

Mum, who helped me with the monumentally stressful task, laughs. "Do you think we have time to grab a coffee before we head back to my sister, the bridezilla?"

I laugh too. "Kate's hardly a bridezilla. It's Cayley you've got to watch out for. And yes to the coffee. I don't care if they need me to do something else, I need sustenance."

She slips her arm through mine and we wander down the road a short way to a small cafe. "I've missed you so much, Jax," she says, smiling wistfully up at me.

"I've missed you too," I say, squeezing her hand.

We order and sit in the courtyard out the back, the afternoon sun making me relaxed and drowsy.

"How have you been?"

"Yeah, I've been all right."

"Really?" She raises her eyebrows to question the honesty of my statement. "I know you've had a pretty tough time."

"Yeah, it was. The breakup with Annie was … rough. But I'm okay now."

"So why are you sleeping at Kate's place instead of David's?"

Ah. I haven't planned this out, with her shock appearance and all. Kate knew she was coming, but they decided to keep it a surprise. And it's a great surprise, but it's really put me on the spot.

I rub at the back of my neck while I struggle to find words. Eventually I give up trying to say something clever and look up at her, shrugging my shoulders and sighing. "I had a fight with his sister."

She purses her lips in thought. "Ellie? No, Emmie?"

"Essie," I say. "Estella."

"Oh." Her eyes go wide as I say her name.

"What?"

She shakes her head and thanks the waitress who's

appeared to deposit our coffees and pastries onto the table. Mum takes a sip immediately and winces. I grin as I realise nothing's changed with her. She will forever burn her tongue on the first sip of coffee. "It was less about her being David's sister and more about her being Estella, wasn't it? This fight you had?"

I lean my head in my hands, elbows propped on the edge of the table. "Maybe," I groan.

"Is it something you can make better?"

I shrug and pick at the danish in front of me. "I don't know. I'm trying, but …"

Mum gives me a gentle smile and reaches across the table to take my hand and prevent me from entirely destroying the food. "I'm glad to hear you're trying."

I blink. "What do you mean?"

"You have a tendency to close yourself off as soon as you have conflict with someone. You let them walk away far too easily."

"You sound like Cayley. Maybe they just find it far too easy to walk away from me." I mutter and take a sip of my coffee, burning my own tongue. I let out a hiss. "I don't really blame them."

"That's … Oh, Jax."

I avoid her gaze, tearing chunks off the pastry and shoving them into my mouth. Eventually she moves away from the subject.

"Will I get to meet Estella?"

"I don't know," I say. "She's supposed to be coming to the wedding, but I'm not sure she will. She … Last time I saw her, she gave me the impression she'd like never to be near me again." I eye her then finally ask the question that's been on my mind since her arrival. "Are you staying after the wedding? Or going back?"

"I don't know," she says. "I had thought I would, but Jax, if you need me here, I'm not going."

"I don't want you to not go because of me," I say, and I'm horrified that my voice is shaking. "You've already put so much on hold for me."

She sighs, and it tugs the corners of her mouth down. "Is that what you think? That I've spent the last twenty years waiting around until I could go and live the life I wanted?"

"I know it's what you always wanted to do," I say, unable to meet her eyes again.

"Yes, when I was seventeen I wanted to go and travel the world, and there's a lot I do want to see, but Jax, honey, plans change. Two months ago I bet you never thought you'd fall in love with Estella."

"I never said anything about being in love with her!"

She waves away my protests. "Not the point. You thought for a long time that you'd be with Annie, but things changed and for the better. Yes, before you arrived I had plans, but they changed. And you're the greatest part of my life. If you need me here Jax – for a few weeks, months, years – then that's where I'll be."

"I don't want to trap you here again." The shaking of my voice is getting worse and there's a hideous prickling behind my eyes.

"Oh, baby, nothing you've ever done has trapped me anywhere. Did you think I just got on that plane and never looked back?"

I give a half-hearted shrug. Mum picks up her phone, lighting up the screen and turning it to face me.

Her background is a collage of photos. All of them of me. She wraps her hands around mine. "Honey, leaving you here, even as an adult, it was the hardest thing I've ever done. I missed you every second I was away."

"But you wanted to go so badly."

"Yeah, I did, and if that ever made you feel like it was easy for me to leave, then I am so, so sorry. Jackson, you are not easy to walk away from. I wonder if maybe you walk away before the other person gets the chance to."

I slump and hit my head against the table with a dull thump. "Now you sound like Essie," I mutter with a groan, recalling the words she threw at me. "I still don't know how to make it right. I said horrible things to her and if she doesn't want to talk to me, isn't it wrong for me to keep pushing her?"

Mum studies me for a long moment, carefully selecting her words. "Do you think she actually wants nothing to do with you, or do you think she's doing exactly what you do, and trying to protect herself from being hurt?"

I think back to New Year's Eve, the way she danced with me, her fingers skimming across my cheek. I think about the afternoon in the kitchen when she kissed me back, offered more.

I remember all the times the brave girl with the wild smile shuttered, guarding herself with anger, cloaking herself in sarcasm. Protecting herself.

Mum nods, no doubt seeing the realisation dawn on my face. "Exactly, Jax. Respect her boundaries, but if she's the right one, prove to her that she can trust you with her heart."

"She is," I say, my voice rough and fragile with the truth. "She's the right one."

She smiles. "I know she is."

"And Mum," I say, riding this wave of truth, "can we talk more about you finishing your trip later, after the wedding?"

As much as it hurts me to be left behind, I'll be okay, because I know she'll always, always come back to me.

Chapter Fifty-One

ESSIE

I FINISH the last stitches on the dress half an hour before I need to leave for the wedding.

Mum has been helping me every minute she's been home since the night we talked in my room. To my surprise, she's been home far more than she normally would be, too. As we've sewed, with me doing the bulk of it and her doing fiddly hand stitching, we've talked, mostly about my business but about other things too, and not only about me. We've talked about her, too, about the vet clinic, about her work, about her dreams. It's a tentative new stage of our relationship and so far I like it.

She's curling my hair while I sit here and finish the last touches with a needle and thread, this part of the project too delicate and finicky to feed through my machine.

"I'm done," I say, laying it in my lap as I snip off the last thread.

It's finished, and it's perfect. The bridesmaid dresses have been the most nerve-wracking project I've worked on, but this dress has been the most technically difficult and the one I love the most, because it's all for me.

"Good," Mum says. "You need to do your makeup."

Forty-five minutes later I pull into the venue. I park and carefully balance on the sky-high silver heels Mum pulled from the back of her wardrobe earlier when I realised I had no shoes that went with the dress. I gaped at her in her ever-sensible jeans, t-shirt and sneakers as she handed over the strappy shoes twinkling with tiny rhinestones.

"I was fun once, you know." She laughed at my expression, then helped me strap them on.

I wobble across the gravel driveway and along the brick path leading to the garden out the back where the ceremony will take place.

I've made sure to arrive right before the start so I don't have to loiter about, making awkward small talk with people I don't know.

I still can't believe they invited me – in fact, they insisted on me coming. I barely know Kate and Cayley, and while Melissa is a friend I didn't think we were all that close. None of her other friends are here.

I find a spot near the front but off to the side, standing in the shade of a tree with a couple of other people. A moment later Travis and his groomsmen appear. One is clearly his brother, or a close relation, based on their resemblance. The other must be a friend of his.

I haven't seen Jax anywhere and I wonder what's keeping him. I do see the woman who arrived in the driveway the other day after I'd dropped off the dresses. She smiles softly at me and gives a little wave when my eyes meet hers. There's something weirdly familiar about her, but I can't figure out why.

The music starts, the celebrant asks the audience to stand and Melissa appears at the end of the aisle.

The dress is a dream. I'm still awestruck that I made it. She glides down the aisle, the satin and chiffon swirling around her feet, a small bouquet of cream roses tied with matching ribbon in her hands.

When she reaches the end Travis kisses her on the cheek and she stands to the side. I turn and Cayley is already partway down the aisle.

If the dress looks good on Melissa, it looks sensational on Cayley. She spots me standing off to the side and gives me a wide grin, her eyes sparkling with what might be tears. She too meets Travis at the end of the aisle before taking her place.

There's a short lull, then everyone turns to the far end of the garden and the bride appears.

I note that she's stunningly gorgeous in a cream gown with bouquets to match the girls', except hers is tied with ribbon to match their dresses, but that's all I see before my eyes land on the person beside her.

Jax.

Jax is walking Kate down the aisle.

He's wearing a suit.

My knees feel weak.

I've seen Jax in his filthy work clothes, the casual clothes he wears around home, half-dressed in pyjama pants and no shirt and dressed nicely, like for Christmas and the New Year's party.

I've loved every version of Jax, from the workshop grime

smudged on his cheek to the easy comfort of t-shirt, jeans and bare feet, to the allure of that well-worn leather jacket.

But this version of Jax, Special Occasion Jax, with his brown hair neat, his face freshly shaven, hands free from grease, in a dark grey suit with crisp white shirt and soft lilac tie: this is my favourite Jax.

He looks nervous. He shakes out his shoulders. It's a subtle movement, but I know him well enough to know it's a little nervous habit of his. He glances at Kate and murmurs something to her. She nods, and they begin to walk.

Kate is beaming at everyone, her smile bright as a sunbeam, her gown absolutely stunning, but it still can't distract me from Jax.

He makes eye contact with the beautiful woman from the driveway and smiles at her. His soft, open smile that I've only ever seen directed at me on the very rare occasion.

She smiles back and her gaze flicks to me, then back to him so quickly I think I've imagined it.

But then Jax's head turns ever so slightly.

Our eyes meet and his mouth drops open, like he's exhaling a long breath. His gaze burns as it travels down my body and back to my face. The corner of his mouth curves up and then he's past me, arriving at the end of the aisle where Travis is waiting.

Cayley is already crying, Melissa handing her tissues from behind their bouquets.

Jax kisses Kate on the cheek and turns away, his eyes finding mine again.

I think he might make his way to me and I wonder if it's rude to run out on someone else's wedding, because I don't think I have it in me to cope with being near Jax while there is a wedding taking place.

He sends one of those smiles in my direction and turns away from me too, going to sit in the front row beside the woman from the driveway.

He wraps an arm around her and she leans into him, resting her head against his shoulder and her hand on his chest. He shifts, looking back over his shoulder, meeting my eyes again, because despite the fact I'm here for a wedding, I can't take my eyes off him.

He smiles, wider this time, and I feel my mouth curling into a smooth curve.

His head tilts then he turns away as the celebrant clears her throat and the wedding begins.

Chapter Fifty-Two

JAX

AS EVERYONE EXPECTED, the wedding is beautiful.

I don't know much about weddings, flowers, dresses or romance of any kind, but the bride was gorgeous, the groom shed a tear or two, the bridesmaid bawled like a two-year-old who'd dropped her ice cream and I didn't trip over my own feet as I escorted my aunt down the aisle. Vows were said, everything sealed with a kiss.

Plus, there was an absolutely stunning girl standing in the shade of a tree. If I turned my head the slightest degree I could make out the shape and colour of her.

By the end of the ceremony I had a serious crick in my neck.

She's wearing the dress. The dress made from that dark pink fabric I saw her cutting out when I first moved in.

The top hugs her body with the fabric wrapping itself around her, emphasising every curve. Half a dozen tiny delicate straps that sparkle like diamonds in the sunlight loop over each shoulder.

The back of the dress barely covers her waist. If I were to

rest my hand in that magic curve between her ribs and hip I'd be able to brush my fingertips across her skin.

Then there's the skirt. Layer upon layer of that fabric that shimmers as she moves. It cascades in soft swirling ruffles to the ground and when she moves it reveals a dramatic split to mid-thigh.

I didn't trip walking Aunt Kate down the aisle, but I nearly fell on my face when I saw that.

The moments immediately following the ceremony were a blur of congratulations for Kate and Travis, guests swarming over Cayley and Melissa to gush over their dresses and the poor photographers trying to corral everyone into group photos.

I stood where I was told, smiled when I was asked to and then was released to do what I wanted while Kate, Travis and the girls went to do their photos.

"So, she came then?" Mum appears by my side after she's released from her own photo duty as sister of the bride.

"Yeah," I breathe, my eyes searching the crowd for the deep pink of Essie's dress.

"Kate told me she made the girls' dresses. I'm assuming she made the one she's wearing."

"Yeah, she did." I'm still searching. I can't see her anywhere. The memory of her cutting out all those pieces of fabric for the skirt flashes through my mind. Essie sitting in the middle of her lounge scowling at me. It brings a smile to my face.

"She's over there." Mum points and I see her standing with Cayley and Melissa, the photographer posing the three of them together. My heart settles, knowing she's still here. Mum nudges me in the shoulder. "Go, now's your chance, catch her before she can disappear again."

"I—"

But she cuts me off. "I don't care if it's your aunt's wedding. Take your chance, Jax." She shoves me harder and I stumble forward.

Most of the guests have dispersed, wandering over to collect drinks or something to eat off a grazing table set up on the balcony of the reception room. Mum heads for Kate and Travis, helping adjust her dress, holding flowers as needed.

Essie is still talking to the girls, helping Cayley wipe away the tear tracks on her face.

I stand nearby and watch.

I watch as Essie smiles and laughs, her movements easy and unrestrained. This is the Essie I remember, with the smile and the sparkle.

She finishes touching up Cayley's face, adjusts something on one of the dresses and turns, but by then I'm already striding away, up the steps and vanishing into the building.

Chapter Fifty-Three

ESSIE

JAX WAS RIGHT THERE and now he's gone.

I saw him from the corner of my eye as I touched up Cayley's makeup after her epic cry during the wedding ceremony.

She was crying so hard the celebrant had to pause for a moment so she could regain her composure.

Her makeup repaired, she heads off for more photos with Melissa and a tall, striking guy she introduced to me as her boyfriend Andrew, and I wander around the gardens.

The ceremony was held late so they could take sunset photos and the sun is already low on the horizon.

I head inside, find a bathroom then a drink, and emerge onto the balcony. Most of the guests are mingling at one end, near the food tables.

I head away from the crowd towards the quiet end that's lit only by a few string lights along the balustrade.

Movement in the shadows has my heart leaping and I startle with a gasp.

"Sorry, I didn't mean to give you a fright."

That voice, a little rough around the edges. It still feels as smooth as ever, sliding over my skin as Jax emerges from the darkness.

"Why're you hiding in the dark?" I blurt.

"Trying to gather my nerve," he says, then trails off. He rubs the back of his neck, his eyes not meeting mine. "I'll, uh, leave you to it," he says as he makes to move past me.

"Jackson," I say, my voice breaking on those two syllables. "Wait." My hand brushes his sleeve and he freezes.

I tip my head back, taking a deep breath. I admire the colour of the sky for a moment, the oranges streaking into pink and up into dusky purple. There's a twinkle and the first star appears.

"Jackson," I say, lowering my chin and looking back to him. My voice shakes but I need to get the words out, regardless of what happens afterwards, even if the wish I fired at that star doesn't come true. I have to say it. "I'm really sorry for what I said. I didn't mean it. I was upset and angry and I made it up."

He exhales, his body deflating as the tension leaks away. "You were right, though."

I shake my head. "No, no I wasn't." I fight back a sob but it still manages to escape me.

"I'll admit, it hurt. It hurt a lot, but since you said it to me, Cayley and my mum have both said something very similar." He smiles ruefully and realisation hits me.

"That's your mum?"

He grins. "Yeah, she came back for the wedding. I had no idea."

"That's why she looks familiar. She looks like you." How did I not see it? I've spent so long staring at Jax's mouth and hers is the exact same shape.

"Well, not really." He rubs the back of his neck. "I look like my dad, apparently."

"No," I say, "there's definitely a lot of her in you. But anyway," I wave my hands in the air, trying to get back to the point of our conversation, "I still wanted to say I'm sorry."

"Estella," he says, then pauses, as if waiting for me to give him permission to use my name, or speak. I raise an eyebrow and he shoots me a little smile before continuing. "God, I'm so sorry." A deep breath. "I don't know how to do this." He gestures between us. "I don't know how to make this right. I'm so scared I'm going to make it worse."

He takes a couple of quick steps and stops right in front of me, pain etched around his eyes in the places his laughter usually sits. "Everything that happened that night. I don't know what happened. I know I hurt you though, and I'm so sorry. I should never have said that about the drama." His voice breaks on the last word.

"You were right, though; I should have spoken to you. It wasn't you who said it. David did."

He shakes his head, like he's clearing away that thought so he can focus on the main thread of the conversation instead of getting distracted by my brother, and I find myself smiling.

"All that stuff," he begins, then hesitates. I watch him and wait. "All that stuff that people have said about you, about you causing drama or whatever, I … I need you to know, all of those things are why I love you so much. I always have. Even when you were only David's sister to me, you were always so fun and sassy and stood up for yourself. You never put up with anything from anyone. I think that's why I was so mad about Jeremy at Melissa's party, because you let him get away with it and you never let anyone else get away with anything. But what other people say is being 'over-dramatic'" – he uses little air quotes around the word – "it's not. There's nothing 'over' about it. It's what makes you so damn amazing." He stops, breathing hard. "So damn amazing," he says again, voice low this time.

It curls around me as I stand there and stare at him, trying to process all the different things he's said in his tirade.

He thinks I'm amazing, he was mad I let Jeremy get away with it, I stood up for myself, David's little sister.

I cringe and deflate. It's back to this, those words I heard him say the day he moved into our house.

She's your kid sister, gross.

"Estella." His voice brings me back to the present. Back from that day when I stood in the hallway and felt tears pricking at my eyes, and decided instead to bury the pain with anger. "I lost you there."

"Look, I get it, okay," I say, my voice heavy. "Thank you for your apology. I'm sorry for what I said and I hope you can forgive me someday. But Jax …" I ignore his wince at my use of the nickname. "I don't think I can be friends with you." My voice trails off in a whisper, more tears blurring my vision of him, standing there in that gorgeous suit with his stupidly lovely tie loosened and crooked.

"What, why?" he asks in a croak.

"Because it doesn't matter how amazing you think I am, I'm just David's little sister to you, and I can't …" I take a deep breath and force myself to finish "… I can't go back to seeing you as only my brother's friend, okay?"

He gapes at me. "Estella, is that all you got from everything I said? My single reference to you being David's sister?"

I nod, lip trembling so hard I don't trust myself to speak.

"Did you entirely miss the part where I accidentally told you I was in love with you?"

"What?" The word is barely a sound, sticking in my throat.

"All of those things, you being bright and bold and brilliant and brave and more than a tiny bit badass, and yes that's a lot of 'b' words, all of those things and so many more things, Estella, all those things that you think people don't like about you … they are all the reasons I love you."

"But—"

"Stop arguing with me. It's the truth. You, Estella, are the brightest burning star. I cannot stop thinking about you, I cannot stop wanting to touch you. Every day I lived in that house with you, Estella, and every single day since."

He's breathless again, gazing at me with those hazel eyes and the soft brown hair, highlighted by the minimal glow of fairy lights.

"I know you might not feel the same, you might not be able to forgive me, or believe me, but I had to tell you. I don't even care what David says about it. That's his problem, not mine, not yours, not ours."

"You love me." It's not a question, it's a reaffirmation, and he nods, resolute but still wary. "You make me feel strong," I whisper, not sure what I'm even saying but knowing he has to know how I feel. "You never make me feel small, or like I'm too much. You don't make me feel weak. Other people, being with them …" My voice trails off as he steps even closer, his toes meeting mine, the skirts of my dress swirling around his thighs. "I felt weak when I was around him; I felt insignificant and weak like I didn't really matter, like I should be small. You've never made me feel like that. With you, I always feel strong, and for that … I love you for that, Jackson." I can't meet his eyes. I can't look at him as he breathes my name at my admission.

He lifts a hand, leaving it hovering right near my face. I can feel the heat of it and my eyes flutter closed.

He doesn't move it any closer, though. "Estella," he murmurs, and I open my eyes, gazing directly into his. He tilts his head in question.

"One hundred percent," I whisper.

His fingers trail across my cheek, palm settling against my skin. Sparks shoot through my veins, my bloodstream filling with a million gold and silver stars. His other hand finds my waist, fingertips grazing the bare skin of my back, and pulls me even closer. Then his lips are brushing mine, my heart taking flight.

He holds me close, oh so close, and kisses me – for minutes, hours, I don't know and I don't care. The wedding could be over and everyone gone home and I wouldn't care, because Jackson Sherwood is kissing me, again and again.

We break apart and he presses a kiss to my forehead before resting his against it, our noses brushing.

I slide my hands up his arms, wrapping them around his neck.

"It's always one hundred percent with you, Jackson."

Acknowledgments

There are many people without whom I could not have written and published this book. I hope I don't forget anyone! If I do, I'm really sorry in advance.

First of all and most of all, thank you to Chris, my amazing husband, who let me go off on this crazy, crazy journey and supported me the whole way, even when I fell into writing holes and didn't emerge for several hours/days/weeks.

To my girls, Charlotte, Taylor and Isabelle: Thank you for enduring my constant distractedness as I researched trim sizes and ISBNs, and for collecting all my book orders from the mailbox. Just think of the muscles you'll have from carrying them all. I love you so much and I hope you grow up to be as sassy and bold as Essie.

Thank you to the rest of my family, especially my parents and siblings. Thanks for getting me to this point and for helping with kids and life and everything else when I was lost in my words.

My besties, betas, sistars (that's not a typo – it's a thing), Kelsey and Natalie: Honestly, there is no way I could have done this without you. (At this point I'm not sure I could do *anything* without you.) You're always there to listen to me rant about a plot hole, writer's block, every single up and down on this rollercoaster ride. I love you forever.

To my friends: How did I get so lucky? Vanessa and Indi for constant, unwavering support and enthusiasm; the Cat Mums; Haley; my Booksta tribe, especially Sarah and Caleb: what would I do without you two? And all my other amazing, incredible friends who've repeatedly asked when they can buy my books: NOW! You can buy this one NOW!

The amazing authors who've helped me along the way: Tammy Robinson, Melissa Guyan, Georgia Peterson, S.J. Pratt, Bellebird James, Tom E. Moffat and the amazing Angela Armstrong. You have all been a goldmine of support and knowledge. New Zealand's writing community is incredible and I'm so honoured to be a part of it.

My editor Patricia Bell and cover designer Jenn Rackham for making this book the best it could be and being so amazing to work with.

For everyone else, whom I've probably forgotten to mention by name: Anyone along the way who has cheered me on, supported me, wanted to buy my books and told their friends I'm a writer, plus all those who've helped me get to this incredible point in my life where my dreams are coming true – I'm forever grateful.

About the Author

Lynda Tomalin lives in a small town in New Zealand, where she writes sweet, swoony books about teenagers finding their place in the world.

She is a mum of three girls and a farmer's wife, and when she's not daydreaming about her fictional characters and trying to find space for all the books she keeps buying, she works in administration (but mostly only to fund making books).

Find her online:
www.lyndatomalinauthor.com
Instagram and Facebook:
@lynda.tomalin.author

Email:
contact@lyndatomalinauthor.com

CPSIA information can be obtained
at www.ICGtesting.com
Printed in the USA
BVHW082250260123
657279BV00004B/64